The
BOY
from
TOMORROW

Camille DeAngelis
Amberjack Publishing
New York | Idaho

Amberjack Publishing
1472 E. Iron Eagle Drive
Eagle, Idaho 83616
http://amberjackpublishing.com

Paperback ISBN: 978-1-948705-20-2

Publisher's Cataloging-in-Publication data originally filed for
hardcover edition:
Names: DeAngelis, Camille, author.
Title: The boy from tomorrow / by Camille DeAngelis. Description:
New York, NY; Eagle, ID: Amberjack Publishing, 2018. Identifiers:
ISBN 978-1-944995-61-4 (Hardcover) | 978-1-944995-62-1
(ebook) | LCCN 2017954150
Summary: Josie and Alec communicate via spirit board, realize they are
living in the same house a century apart, and develop a life-changing
friendship.
Subjects: LCSH Psychics--Juvenile fiction. | Spiritualism--Juvenile
fiction. | Friendship--Juvenile fiction. | Ghosts--Juvenile fiction. |
Child abuse--Juvenile fiction. | Family--Juvenile fiction. |Ghost stories.
| BISAC JUVENILE FICTION / Ghost Stories |JUVENILE
FICTION / General
Classification: LCC PZ7.D351 Bo 2018 | DDC [Fic]--dc23

Cover Design & Illustrations: Agnieszka Grochalska

For Elliot & Kate,
who said,
Think of all the people we'll love
who haven't been born yet.

Josie Asks the Oracle
1.

A companion is not always the same as a friend. Josie's sister was her closest—indeed, her *only*—companion, but a little sister is too young to understand certain things, like the concept of privacy, for instance, or the crucial role of books in the development of a person's intelligence. Josie's tutor understood such things, as well she should, but then, her tutor was nearly a decade older—a grown woman, if a bit of a goose at times.

No, Josie Clifford required a *friend:* someone her own age, who knew what it was to be lonely, who would not call her morbid when she confided that she sometimes awoke cold and trembling in the middle of the night, convinced that she would not live to her sixteenth birthday. That was something you could never, *ever* tell your little sister.

On one such night, when sleep had abandoned her, Josie lit a candle and tiptoed down the stairs to her mother's reading room. There were books in the reading room, but her mother seldom took any out of the glass-fronted cabinet. A very different sort of "reading" happened here most weekday afternoons, when Mrs. Clifford convinced strangers she could speak to the dead.

There were curious things inside the cabinet and along the side table, mostly gifts from Mr. Berringsley, who was her mother's best client. There was a talking board with angels painted at the corners, a crystal ball that grew tinglingly warm when you touched it, and a contraption through which—were you brave enough to fix the earpiece to your ear—you could hear the voices of your ancestors telling you where you ought to travel and whom you ought to marry in order to fulfill your destiny. Josie didn't truly believe it was possible to speak with your ancestors, or angels, or people who died in tragic accidents, and yet she always found herself sneaking back into this dark and eerie room as if she did.

Her favorite of Mr. Berringsley's gifts was a brass sculpture, perhaps ten inches tall, in the shape of a woman in a flowing cape. The hooded figure had downcast eyes and hands outstretched above a glass panel, which displayed the mechanism that stacked and shuffled a set of cards. (The *real* oracles of ancient Greece did not need fortune cards, her tutor Emily had pointed out, but Mr. Berringsley's sphere was finance, not history.) When you pressed the button at the base, the device chose a fortune for you. Josie had longed to press that button when Mr. Berringsley first presented the gift a month ago, but she had known better than to ask her mother if she might. Mother always, *always* said no—but Mother was not here now.

"I wish for a true friend," Josie whispered. How ridiculous that her heart should race as she laid her finger on the button! There was no magic here, after all.

The mechanism whirred to life, and the two stacks of cards wove in and out before one fortune slid forward. Josie held her candle to the glass.

You shall be united with the object of your desire.

Part of her—the *foolish* part—was delighted. It was easy to believe in false prophets. She must ask a second question to test it.

"Does my mother love me?" Josie said, and pressed the button again. This time the card read:

It is not meant to be.

Josie saw then that she had placed herself in a distressing predicament: whether or not the oracle machine proved true, happiness would only ever be allotted to her in half measure. She did not dare ask again.

H-E-L-L-O S-P-I-R-I-T

2.

It was almost as if the new house—an *old* house—had a personality of its own; it was calm and quiet and generous, happily divulging its secrets one at a time so long as Alec asked nicely. The real estate agent told them that someone famous, an actress maybe, had built the place a hundred years ago. People had been happy here, lived *interesting* lives in these rooms, and now it was their turn.

Alec was born in the city, but after one perfect week in the Adirondacks when he was five, he'd wanted very badly to wake up to birdsong and the soft sound of the wind in the trees, not just on vacation, but *every* morning. The clamor of the city made him anxious, and while his mother understood this, it had taken several years of conversations about moving before it actually happened.

And then, after all that, his father did not move with them. The house at 444 Sparrow Street was much too big for a family of two, though neither Alec nor his mother would ever admit it. The divorce was painful enough.

But this new-old house would comfort them, even as his mother arranged for the necessary repairs and renovations. Mrs. Frost was starting a new job soon at the elementary school, and Alec would be able to walk to the middle school. Surely there were two or three friends to be made in this leafy-green neighborhood.

In the meantime, he had the whole house to explore. There were cupboards, each peculiar in its own way: a huge curio cabinet in the dining room, a storage nook on the landing midway up the front stairs, and a small one, the size of a medicine cabinet, built into the wall of the spare room adjoining his new bedroom. It had an old-fashioned keyhole but no key, and Alec's mother was too busy talking to the contractor about the new back porch to pay much notice to this little mystery.

"Don't you want to know what's inside?" Alec asked.

"Probably nothing," Mrs. Frost replied.

"Then why would it be locked?"

She smiled as if she were happy again. "There *is* such a thing as too much imagination, you know."

Alec ran his fingers over the woodwork. The cupboard had been painted over a half-dozen times, and sloppily too, so that the shape of the keyhole was no longer crisp. Maybe the key was lost somewhere in the house.

The contractor gave him a battered wooden crate full of things the workmen had found behind the walls and under the floorboards: a fistful of rusty jacks, crumbling wads of newspaper, broken bits of fancy china, a book so moldy he couldn't make out the title. Alec rummaged eagerly, but the only key in the box was a boring modern one. The house was holding onto this secret for the time being.

But it offered him another one: a talking board. Alec found it in the massive curio cabinet in the dining room, in a drawer that stuck so badly most people would have given up tugging on it.

The board was laid out in black and gold on a wooden tray about eighteen inches square. There was an angel in each corner carrying a banner: HELLO in the top left, GOODBYE on the right, and on the bottom, YES and NO. The alphabet was arranged in a pair of concentric circles at the center of the board, A through M on the outside and N through Z on the inside, with a question mark at the center. The numbers appeared in a row along the bottom edge, with TODAY and TOMORROW on either side. Carefully, Alec lifted the board out of the drawer and found a glass pointer in a niche lined with green felt.

It was the coolest thing he'd ever seen, no contest. Alec wanted to call out to his mother, but something made him pause. He might be the only living person who knew about this, and it would be fun to keep it that way for a day or two.

He Googled "spooky board with letters" and found that people used them to try to communicate with the dead. You'd put your fingers on the glass pointer—the planchette—and ask a question, and the ghost would supposedly push the pointer from letter to letter to answer you. He wondered how often the board had been used by its original owner, and he shivered at the next thought that came to him: *you could ask.*

Their new neighbors stopped by with welcome gifts, things like pineapples and homemade mulberry jam. Two of the women had sons in Alec's grade, and this was how he came to host a sleepover before school had even started.

Alec was nervous, but Danny put him at ease. The boy came barreling through the front door, laughing and joking, as if he were already planning to spend a great deal of time here in the years to come. He told Alec's mom her homemade pizza was "an edible masterpiece," and Alec watched another of those rare-these-days smiles light up her face.

Danny's friend Harold was quiet in comparison. After dinner he passed a few minutes browsing Alec's bookshelves, saying eventually, "You sure like Terry Pratchett."

"*Discworld* is the *best*," Danny put in, and Harold arched a brow.

"*The* best?"

"Who's your favorite writer?" Alec asked.

Harold shrugged. "Hemingway, maybe. Or Vonnegut."

Danny laughed and turned to Alec. "He just picks authors who sound the most impressive."

Watching a movie seemed like a safer bet than talking about books, so Alec suggested they go downstairs again, and they settled on *The Incredibles*.

Once Mrs. Frost had gone up to bed, Alec led his new friends to the dining room and opened the drawer. Danny ran his finger along the board's golden outlines while Harold hefted the planchette in his palm.

"Handpainted," Danny said admiringly. "Definitely one of a kind."

Danny's father owned the antiques store on Main Street, and over pizza he'd talked about the weird old stuff his dad had found in dead people's houses.

"Have you ever used one?" Alec asked as they sat down at the dining table.

"First time for everything," Danny replied. "But I know how. I saw it on TV once. So who are we trying to talk to?"

"What about Einstein? Or Houdini? No, I've got it," Harold laughed, "Attila the Hun!"

"If we actually talked to Attila the Hun, you wouldn't understand a word he said," Danny pointed out. He drew a pad and pencil out of his backpack. "Here, you guys put your fingers on it, and I'll write down the letters."

Harold laid the pointer on the board and pushed it with his index finger. It looked like a plain old paperweight. The glass was slightly concave, magnifying each letter it rested on, the edge rimmed in green felt to protect the wooden surface.

"If it even works," Harold said. "Which it won't."

Danny turned to a fresh page and waited.

"Hello?" Alec said, starting when the lamp in the corner flickered. Harold laughed.

"Look!" Danny said. "It's moving!"

The glass piece made a whispering sound as it glided across the board. Unseen hands directed the pointer to HELLO in the upper left corner, then moved back to the circles of letters:

S-P-I-R-I-T

They glanced at one another with raised eyebrows.

"Who are you?" Alec asked, and the glass piece took off again:

W-E A-R-E Y-O-U-N-G L-A-D-I-E-S

The boys spoke over each other as they sounded out the words. Danny scribbled it down, and when he was done, Alec asked, "How many of you are there?"

The pointer dipped to the number three.

AND HOW MANY OF YOU?

"There are three of us, too." Alec's hands were shaking, and he hoped the others wouldn't notice. Harold couldn't be pushing the glass—if he were, the pointer would already be spelling out "your mom" jokes.

"When did you die?" Danny asked. "Were you murdered?"

CERTAINLY NOT—a pause—WE ARE VERY MUCH
ALIVE—

Harold laughed again. "That's what they all say."

THE PLANCHETTE SPINS—WHAT DOES THIS
SIGNIFY?

The marker had only moved to point to each letter in turn. "What do you mean?" Alec asked. "It's not spinning."

IT HAS STOPPED NOW—DO YOU MEAN TO SAY YOU
SEE THE BOARD—DO YOU SEE US, SPIRIT?

"Not gonna lie, you guys," Danny whispered. "I am getting a little freaked."

Fear surged through Alec's fingertips, yet he felt himself carried along by it. How could they stop now? "We can't see you. Can you see us?"

WE CANNOT—BUT YOU SAY YOU SEE OUR BOARD?

9

"We see *our* board."

YOUR BOARD?

Then the pointer began to whirl in a circle, and the boys jumped back from the table. Harold muttered a curse, and Alec's heart hammered in his chest. Now the glass piece moved between the letters even though no one was touching it, and Danny scrambled for his pencil.

SILLY STUBBORN SPIRITS—

"We're not the spirits!" Alec cried. "*You* are!"

Then the planchette made a quick series of sidesteps in the bottom right corner:

NO NO NO. YOU ARE QUITE MISTAKEN—GOOD-NIGHT SPIRIT—

Alec looked at the other boys in turn, not knowing what to say. Even Harold, who seemed quick to laugh at anything he didn't understand, sat back from the table, folded his arms, and stared at the board.

"All right," Danny said finally. "Which of you was pushing it?"

Josie's Wish is Granted
3.

Josie leaned back from the table, her pulse pounding in her ears. Cassie gazed at her with saucer eyes, more frightened than her sister had ever seen her. Emily rose and whisked the talking board back into the drawer. She paced the carpet a few times, chuckled nervously, and proffered her hands so the girls could see how she trembled.

"Would you look at me! I could never do what your mother does for a living."

"Mother doesn't *really* talk to spirits." This was the first time Josie had ever said so aloud, and the declaration settled her nerves.

"What do you call this, then?"

Josie bit her lip. It was impossible that Cassie could

have manipulated the planchette, for it had formed words her sister didn't know how to spell. When the pointer strung together "*when did you die*," a horrible thrill had coursed all through her.

Emily shook her head. "Until tonight I'd have said you two were capable of any mischief—but not this, certainly not this."

"I can't explain it," Josie said.

"Perhaps your mother could, were any of us foolish enough to tell her." Now Emily was scurrying around the reading room tidying up the cushions to make it appear as if no one had been there. "Now, then, up to bed. They'll be home soon."

As she hung her dress in the wardrobe, Josie heard Mr. Berringsley's motorcar draw up to the curb. Cass ran to the window seat and looked out.

"He's coming inside," she announced in a stage whisper as three figures—Berringsley, Lavinia Clifford, and Merritt, her manservant—came up the walk. Berringsley spoke, and they heard their mother laugh.

It was Berringsley who'd commissioned the talking board from an artisan in New Orleans. He was a nice man, always well-intentioned, but his enthusiasm gave rise to an awkwardness that only he could not perceive. When he wished to converse with Josie, he drew too near, and his breath made her think of a sealed-off room.

The front door opened and shut, the voices and footsteps moving into the reading room directly beneath the nursery. The murmur of their conversation drifted upward as Emily seated herself at the foot of Cassie's bed, listening with head bowed as the girls said their prayers.

"We pray for those we have loved and see no more," Josie began.

Cassie bent over her tightly clasped hands, eyes screwed tight. When you are six years old, religious devotion and the melodramatic appearance of it are one and the same. "For Grandmother and Grandfather, for Daddy and Mr. Malcolm," she said.

Every night it gave Josie a prickly feeling along the back of her neck to hear her little sister mention their fathers by name. David Malcolm had been Josie's father, but she could not remember him. She'd passed his portrait in the hall every day for years before she even realized who he was.

Mr. Clifford had been kind to Josie—he'd even adopted her—but when he'd come home from a business trip to Panama with some horrible wasting illness, they'd hidden him away, and neither of the girls had been permitted to say goodbye. Not that Cassie would have understood; she wasn't even two.

This was the real reason Josie held no faith in her mother's celebrated ability to commune with the dead. She never spoke of Mr. Malcolm. She never spoke of Mr. Clifford. If their mother had a genuine connection to the spirit world, then why was there never any word from their fathers?

Yet something always compelled Josie to listen for a revelation, shining and definitive, that would prove her right *or* wrong. There were two doors to the reading room—the front hall door and the back door opening onto the kitchen corridor—and sometimes Josie would steal down the back stairs and put her eye to the keyhole to watch her mother's performance. The reading room was her stage: black curtains blotting out the daylight, the old-fashioned lantern lit on the mantelpiece, the smell of sandalwood incense, and all the waiting and hoping inside the silence. The bereaved—

those who had lost someone—were always an ideal audience.

Mrs. Clifford would close her eyes. Her pale hands would quiver, her eyelids fluttered, her head lolled to one side, and when she spoke again it was in the booming tones of a gentleman who claimed to have lived in the lost city of Atlantis a hundred thousand years ago, or another who had been a celebrated poet in Renaissance Italy, or someone—some*thing*—that had never lived at all.

But on other occasions it was as if the spirits merely crept up behind her and whispered in her ear. Even when a person traveled three days by train—so that no one in Edwardstown could have heard anything of their private tragedies—Josie's mother always knew. She told the whereabouts of lost fortunes and the bones of missing children. Of thieves and villains in the sitter's own family. And for every mourner, out of a hundred different ways a person could die, Mrs. Clifford always named the right one: a nasty tumble down the basement stairs. Arsenic poisoning. Tuberculosis.

Last week an elderly lady had come wanting to speak with her dead husband. Her face was cold and sharp, as if she'd never laughed once in all her life, but when Mrs. Clifford spoke the nickname of an old sweetheart—lost at sea nearly fifty years before—the old woman crumpled in her chair and sobbed for a good quarter of an hour, and everyone in the house had had to pretend as if they couldn't hear it.

Mrs. Clifford was clever enough to fool everyone who asked for a spirit reading, but the message through the talking board couldn't *possibly* have been her doing. Josie lay in bed, her confusion compounding itself with each passing moment, while Emily tucked Cassie in.

But when their tutor whispered, "Sleep well, dear ones," the accumulated shadow of strangers, living and not, slithered back into the mouse-holes, and everything felt warm and certain once more. Emily pulled the pins from her hair and it tumbled down her back, gleaming in the moonlight from the side window. Her bedroom adjoined the nursery.

Cassie sat up in bed, her ancient rag doll cuddled under her chin. "Can we talk to the not-alive boys again tomorrow?"

"Oh, Cass. You know that's impossible. Even if it were a good idea—and you know it isn't—your mother hardly ever goes out to dinner. You mightn't get another chance for months."

Josie propped herself on her elbow. "How do you know they're boys?"

"They said so," Cassie replied.

"No, they didn't."

"Come, now," said Emily. "Put it out of your heads, or you won't sleep a wink."

A Message on the Windowsill
4.

The house yielded another secret, and another. Mrs. Frost handed her son a cardboard envelope, stamped "Fairleigh Brothers Studio" in gold at the bottom right corner, and he lifted the flap.

The girl smiled up at him as if she'd looked straight through the lens into the future. It was a sad smile, no parting of the lips, but her pale eyes seemed alight with secret knowledge. Her hair was pulled softly away from her face with a ribbon, and it fell, barely tamed, down her shoulders.

"Her name is Josephine," Mrs. Frost observed. "She looks like she's about your age." As Alec looked at the photograph he was aware of his mother's eyes on him—amused, maybe, that he found the portrait even more interesting than she'd expected him to. "The contractor gave us two more boxes of bits and pieces to look through, and the photo was right on top," she went on. "Maybe you can invite Danny over for a little armchair archaeology."

Alec noticed the handwritten caption in the bottom right corner—*Josephine Clifford, 1915*—along with the photographer's signature.

"Do you think she lived here?"

"I hope she did," Mrs. Frost replied. "She has a kind face." He handed back the portrait, and his mother bent open the front flap and propped it on the mantelpiece. "I like the idea of her looking over us, like a benevolent spirit."

He went upstairs thinking of the girl in the picture. *A benevolent spirit.* Of course she must be dead by now—she'd be more than a hundred and ten otherwise—and yet it seemed preposterous, somehow, that those eyes could be closed forever.

Danny showed up that afternoon wearing a headlamp with an attached magnifying glass sticking out at an angle, so it bounced up and down as he bounded into the kitchen. "You got stuff for sandwiches, Mrs. Frost? Archaeological work sure makes a guy hungry."

Alec's mother suppressed a smile. "I'll have something fixed for you by the time you're finished with your investigations."

"Your mom's a good cook," Danny said as he and Alec went up the back stairs. "Harold didn't like that fake cheese on the pizza, but that's Harold for you."

Alec felt himself getting red in the face. His mother had gone all out with that pizza, dough from scratch and caramelized onions and everything. Harold was a jerk.

"That's the kind of stuff we eat now," he said as they climbed the steps to the attic. "My mom says if you've got to make two huge life changes, you might as well make three."

Danny shrugged. "*I* thought it tasted delish."

"Good, 'cause you're getting Tofurky in your sandwich," Alec laughed.

Alec had carried the two wooden crates of old stuff up the back stairs to the attic, which seemed like a good place to sort through them. He knew from movies that people tended to hide their worst secrets in basements, whereas attics could be bright places where you might discover old and wonderful things. This attic was divided into four rooms, but all of them were empty. If you turned right at the top of the stairs, you'd find an open corridor with three doors along it— these were the old servants' quarters, and each room was small and spare, with flaking white paint and built-in shelves for the servants' belongings. The other side of the attic floor was one long room overlooking the street, and this was where the treasures should have been.

Danny banged the door open and peered hopefully inside. "There are only a few boxes of old stuff," Alec said. "Better than nothing, I guess."

"Some people are just *too tidy*," Danny replied as he settled himself cross-legged on the dusty floor. Alec sat down beside him, and they began drawing items out of the boxes one at a time: more moldy books, a Gumby doll, a tiny spinning top all rusted over. Alec wanted to talk about the talking board, but he didn't want to admit that he hoped it was for real until Danny confessed as much himself.

Danny positioned the magnifying glass in front of his face (making one eye look enormous) as he read the newspaper aloud, advertisements for "cocaine toothache drops" and the "Venus-Adonis electric normalizer" that made Alec laugh. It felt so good to laugh that he went on for longer than the joke really warranted, which made *Danny* laugh, and then it seemed for a minute or so that they might never stop.

It was stiflingly hot up there, and the windows looking out over the street were warped with age. Alec tugged at one sash while Danny, with a weird little smile on his face, wiped away the dust on the next sill over. "I don't *believe* it," he said.

Alec came over to look. Carved into the sill with clumsy strokes were the words *HELLO ALEC.*

"Did you . . .?" he began, but he knew Danny hadn't done it. Decades' worth of dust had filled in the gouges in the wood. A strange feeling trickled over him, as if he were being watched. All along he'd felt as if the house were communicating with him, and wasn't this proof of it?

"It's *them*," Danny whispered.

"Who?" Alec asked, even though he knew.

"The spirits." There was a conspiratorial gleam in Danny's eyes. "The ones we talked to through the board."

"What if it's a coincidence?"

But Alec wanted it *not* to be a coincidence. He wanted this greeting to be meant for him, not for some other Alec who had lived here years and years ago. From the foot of the attic stairs his mother called their sandwiches were ready, and Danny gave h look before darting for the door. Alec paused, passing his fingers one more time over the letters. *You knew my name*, he thought. *Now you have to tell me yours.*

Tea and Gossip
5.

When the bell chimed, Josie reminded herself to descend the stairs at her usual pace.

Mrs. Pike was answering the door as she turned the corner on the first landing. Josie came forward and the housekeeper retreated silently to the kitchen.

"Hello, Josie!" Mabel took her hand and held it out as if to admire her. "That dress is *so* becoming. Did you get it in New York?"

Josie nodded, flushing slightly. "Mother had it made for me."

"And that ribbon in your hair—it matches perfectly."

Josie's fingers flew to the crimson bow Emily had tied for her. It felt strange to be complimented by someone like Mabel, who had the blonde curls and lustrous skin of a china doll.

"Thank you. Shall we go out to the garden?"

Mabel nodded, but her eyes lingered on the door to the reading room, which was shut, even though Mrs. Clifford never saw clients on a Sunday. Josie could hear her mother at the typewriter in the study directly across the hall. Her guest followed her down the corridor to the back of the house, a trifle reluctantly.

"Oh, how enchanting!" Mabel said as they passed through the circle hedge, which was cut into quarters by pathways leading from each direction to the fountain and tea table. Sparrows hopped along the fountain rim, dipping their tiny beaks into the water and chirping away to each other. The air was warm and scented with honeysuckle. Josie's guest was looking all around her—at the fountain, the tree line at the bottom of the yard, the perfectly laid bricks forming the patterned terrace underfoot. "No one can overhear us here," she said with a smile of satisfaction. "We can see everyone who comes and goes."

Someone giggled from behind the hedge. "Not everyone," Josie sighed.

Cassie stood up, her favorite doll nestled in the crook of her arm, and pointed at Mabel. "*You* must be Mabel Foley."

"Why, you charming little thing! She looks just like you, Josie. How old are you, dear?"

"I'm Cassie, and I'm six," the girl said proudly, and held up her plaything. "And this is Mrs. Gubbins." The doll had seen much cleaner days. One of her black button eyes had come loose and dangled below the other, giving her the air of a madwoman. "Mrs. Gubbins tells me everybody else's secrets," Cassie informed their guest. "Mine are the only ones she keeps." No one could remember how Mrs. Gubbins had come into Cassie's possession. There was no one from whom she might have inherited it.

The little girl skipped around the hedge and went to one of the empty chairs, pulling it with a grating noise across the brick and arranging her doll on the seat.

"No," Josie said. "This tea is for Mabel and me. You're to have yours inside."

"But it isn't fair! Mother won't let *me* invite any friends over . . ."

You don't have *any friends*, Josie thought. Neither of them did, really, though she hoped that would change after today.

"But I never get to have a real tea party!"

Mabel smiled indulgently. "Come here, Cassie. Will you find somewhere else to play if I give you something, just for you?" Cassie nodded eagerly as Mabel loosened the drawstring of her purse and took out a caramel. "It's my last one, and it's all for you."

Cassie picked up her filthy doll and skipped away, chewing happily. The screen door slammed, and they waited as Mrs. Pike crossed the lawn and began to set the table. The ham-and-cucumber sandwiches were neatly quartered on the diagonal. There was a plate of fresh scones, crocks of butter and currant jam, and a plate of frosted cakes from the Main Street bakery. Josie sighed with pleasure as Mrs. Pike gathered her tray and went back into the house.

"I'm so glad we met at the park last week," her guest began. "You don't know how often I've passed by your house and wondered about you."

"*Me?*"

"Your mother too, of course. She's quite the figure of mystery around town."

Josie looked at her plate. *This again.*

"Is it true what they say, that her 'spirit control' was a royal physician on the lost continent of Atlantis?"

"That's what she says." Josie's mother was a star, cold and remote. This felt like asking her to comment on something she knew nothing about.

Mabel's eyes grew wide. "You mean you don't believe her?"

"I'm not saying I don't," she replied, for it would not do to admit her skepticism openly. "But she isn't as interesting as she'd have you believe."

"You don't care for your mother?" Mabel seemed amused. "I'm sure you'd get along better if she'd only send you to school. I know I'd go batty if I had to stay cooped up with *my* mother all day." The girl gave Josie an odd look—half sympathetic, half appraising. "Sometimes I see your mother around town in Mr. Berringsley's motorcar, but you're never with her. You don't leave the house much, do you?"

"Mother always says we're safest at home."

"Why shouldn't you be safe anywhere? There's no crime to speak of in Edwardstown, and I should know—my uncle is chief of police, and he spends all day reading the newspaper." As Mabel spoke, Josie picked up the teapot and poured them each a cup. "But I suppose it's all to do with that horrid thing that happened to you the last time you lived here."

Josie shot her a wary glance. "You know about it?"

"Why, everyone does. My uncle assures me it was an isolated incident. Certainly nothing like it has ever happened before, or since." She leaned forward, lowering her voice as if someone else might be hiding behind the hedge. "That man—he said your mother had cheated him out of his inheritance, is that right?"

Josie nodded, sighing inwardly. There was no way

out of this conversation but through it.

"But it was all perfectly legal, so I heard. The man's uncle—Horace Vandegrift?—he'd already changed his will, long before he actually died. Of perfectly sound mind, they say."

Josie didn't like to think about that time, the summer after Mr. Clifford died, when they were living in the house on the other end of town. First the man came to the door while her mother was with a client. He demanded to see her, and when Mrs. Pike denied him he rushed at her, screaming that Lavinia Clifford had bewitched his uncle and cheated him out of his rightful fortune. Josie watched from the nursery window as the police came and took him away.

Two months later, they were out for a stroll in the park—she and her mother and Cassie and Cassie's nurse—and the man, the Vandegrift nephew, sprang out of nowhere. She still remembered the vicious look on his face, and how the knife in his hand glinted in the sunlight. The nurse seized Cassie and ran shrieking across the lawn, and Josie was left alone to watch her mother struggling against the madman. He stabbed her twice, above and below her collarbone, before a policeman could overtake him.

Other things happened afterward. Waking in the middle of the night to the sound of men's voices in the front yard—a brick flung through the dining-room window at breakfast (she remembered how the broken glass shimmered on the oriental carpet)—and a white dress, soaked in pig's blood, left in a sodden heap on the welcome mat. It seemed Mark Vandegrift had friends who felt equally entitled and equally cheated.

All of this was why her mother had taken the dour Scotsman into her employ, and why they no longer lived in the house Cassie's father had bought for them. As soon as she was well enough, Lavinia Clifford used part of her inheritance from Horace Vandegrift to purchase a house that did not yet exist, and while they waited for it to be built they'd gone to live for a time in Manhattan. There was never any question of leaving Edwardstown, for Mr. Berringsley had always lived there, and he was far too generous a patron.

Mabel stirred a dollop of milk into her tea and added two lumps of sugar. "Your mother must have told Mr. Vandegrift some extraordinary things."

Josie nodded. "She made him even richer."

"You've got nothing to worry about now, though, have you? Hasn't the nephew gone to prison?"

"He's in prison, yes. For now."

Her meaning was lost on her companion. "And your mother—was she as gravely injured as everyone says?"

"I don't know. We weren't allowed to see her."

Cassie came skipping back to the tea table. "I'm hungry." Josie handed her a sandwich and nudged her away again.

"And what can you tell of her servant? You know what they say about him, don't you?"

Josie shook her head. She could see how Mabel relished this—turning the gossip back on its subject, or near enough.

"They say he's inhuman. Like some sort of dead thing she's brought back to life"—here Mabel leaned forward and lowered her voice to an excited whisper—"to do her *bidding*."

Josie laughed. "My mother isn't as mysterious as everyone seems to think she is—not by a mile." A picture loomed up: of her mother as a wild-haired voodoo priestess dressed in a mantle of feathers, wearing an alligator-skin belt studded with tiny dolls all stuck through with pins. She laughed again.

"I do wonder, though," said Mabel. "Perhaps there are things you've never noticed."

Josie lifted an eyebrow. "Such as?"

"Where does he sleep? What does he eat? Does he sit for meals with the other servants?"

"I don't know."

"Perhaps he doesn't eat. Perhaps he doesn't sleep."

Josie rolled her eyes. "Tosh!"

Cassie was turning in circles on the lawn, faster and faster, her face lifted to the sky. Mrs. Gubbins sat in the grass looking on. A moment later the girl collapsed on the ground, giggling to herself as if there could be no better company.

"He's awfully strange," said Mabel. "You can't tell me he doesn't give you the creeps."

"Of *course* he gives me the creeps," Josie countered, but Mabel shushed her, and Josie glanced over her shoulder. Her mother and Merritt were coming down the back steps, arm in arm. The man looked even more like a corpse in the cheerful afternoon light. Mabel dabbed at her lips with a corner of her napkin.

"Hello, Mother," Josie said, when they had come near enough for greetings. "Hello, Merritt."

Merritt nodded to each of them. He did not speak, and his eyes were fixed on the tea table as if he were looking straight through it, at something no one else could see. Josie heard Mabel shifting uneasily in her chair.

"You girls have hardly touched your sandwiches," Mrs. Clifford observed. "And I suppose your tea's gone cold, too, with all your chitchatting."

"Oh, no, ma'am," Mabel said brightly, taking a sip to

illustrate.

Josie's mother regarded her guest with an unreadable look. "We'll leave you to your tea party. Make yourself at home, dear."

"Thank you, Mrs. Clifford," Mabel replied, but the pair had already passed beyond the garden room. Cassie was still sprawled on the lawn like a rag doll, and they strode by her as if she were invisible. They were heading down to the back gate, where there was a path that cut between the back lawns of Sparrow and Thrush Streets and led to the graveyard on the hill. Mrs. Clifford sometimes walked in the afternoon, but she never went with anyone but Merritt.

"I can't imagine he provides much in the way of conversation," Mabel said.

"We've gone weeks without hearing him speak." Josie picked up a sandwich, took a bite, and found she was no longer hungry.

"Perhaps that's part of her magic." Mabel split open a scone and buttered it lavishly. "Perhaps he can only speak when she's spoken to him first."

Emily rejoined them for dinner that evening. Josie wanted to tell her about the tea party, but she knew better than to speak of it now.

There was a pause once Emily had told of her afternoon activities in Greenwich Village, and Mrs. Clifford flicked a glance at Josie as she cut her veal into dainty pieces. "How was your visit with the Foley girl?"

"Her name is Mabel." Her mother merely lifted an eyebrow. "It was very nice." Josie hesitated. "Thank you."

"You had the perfect day for it," said Emily.

Her mother paused. "I hope your little tea party

has satisfied your desire for—how did you put it—'outside company'? I do not wish the Foley girl to enter my house again."

Josie's jaw dropped. "But why? What did she do?"

"She's a common snoop, Josephine, and you know it." Her mother went on cutting her veal as if they were discussing the weather. "Don't tell me you didn't see her eyes roving over the place, taking everything in, every word you said, filing it away for her next tea party. When the time comes, dear, don't wonder why you aren't invited."

Josie felt the fire rising in her cheeks. She glanced at Emily, who gave her a sympathetic look. Cassie, seemingly oblivious, swirled her mashed potatoes into a small mountain with her fork and studded it with peas.

"Mabel had never been here before." Josie heard the petulance in her own voice, and it made her more so. "She was just curious."

"It was the wrong kind of curiosity." Her mother sniffed. "Someday you'll understand. Gossip is currency among that lot."

How she hated this. It wasn't fair that a word of criticism from her mother's lips could distort a thing that had been, at the time, almost perfectly enjoyable. "*What* lot?"

"Why, common women! This silly little town is rife with them." Her mother took a sip of wine, glanced at Josie, and sighed. "Of course you don't notice these things. This is why I've kept you out of the day school. Girls don't learn anything useful at a place like that. Your Mabel Foley couldn't spell 'arithmetic,' much less perform any. No," she went on, as if she needed or wanted to convince anyone, "those girls only learn the value, such as it is, of gossip."

"Then why did you even let me invite her?"

"To teach you an important lesson." So Mrs. Clifford had known what Mabel Foley wanted, and she'd let Josie invite her anyway. Her mother had made a fool of her. "Don't sulk, Josephine. Miss Jasper allows you to make your own mistakes, and you forgive her every time."

Now Cassie squashed her mashed-potato mountain into a mesa. "Can I ask a question?"

"I don't know, dear," said Mrs. Clifford. "*Can* you?"

Cassie went on, in her airy childish way, as if she hadn't been corrected. "If it's a silly little town, Mother, then why do we live here?"

"Because it's the silly little people who put the veal on our table."

"The silly little people who think Mother talks to spirits," Josie offered, keeping one eye on Mrs. Clifford's face to gauge her reaction, but Cassie spoke again before their mother could respond.

"Is Mr. Berringsley a silly little person, too?" The girl pushed her plate away, crossed her arms and leaned forward on the table, grinning like an imp.

Josie watched a knot form in her mother's jaw. "Come here, Cassandra."

Every trace of mirth fell from Cassie's face as she got to her feet and rounded the dining table, eyes on the carpet. Mrs. Clifford slapped her daughter on the cheek, leaving an angry red mark, and pointed a long white finger at her nose.

"That's for your impertinence. Now go back to your seat and eat your potatoes, or you will finish them for breakfast."

Other People's Secrets
6.

Some nights it was impossible to fall asleep. He'd start thinking about how horribly different life was now, that even if his dad was working all the time at least Alec knew he'd be home again eventually. As long as his parents were married, Alec's father could be away but he was still *there*, still belonging to them—and now he never would again.

This was a whole new kind of loneliness. Some nights Alec very nearly convinced himself there was someone else in the room with him, someone who didn't want him to know they were there. Maybe there was more than one of them. It was like each doubt and angry thought had gathered itself out of the darkest corners of the bedroom and stood skulking in a circle around his bed. *You're shy. Shyness is weakness. Things bother you that don't bother anybody else and that makes you DIFFICULT. You don't like to play football or baseball, or any of the other things Dad was good at when he was a kid, things he always thought he'd get to do with a son of his own.* Eventually Alec would nod off, and if he woke up an hour or two later the phantoms were gone, but the feelings were still there.

Alec didn't tell his mother about the shadow-people in his room. He knew she'd worry about him even more than she already did, and anyway, he knew perfectly well they weren't really there. "I'm going to make an appointment for you to see someone," she'd said more than once over the past few weeks. "A counselor. So you can talk about your feelings—about the way things are now."

He couldn't see how talking to a stranger would help him to feel any better, but he also wasn't about to say no to anything his mother suggested. Even when he did everything he could think of to please her, she might burst into tears.

The weekend after school started, Danny and Harold spent the night to celebrate Alec's birthday. Alec was still annoyed that Harold had dissed his mother's pizza, but Danny wanted him to come, so Alec resolved to give him another chance. Mrs. Frost made veggie burgers with French fries and a double-chocolate cake.

"Maybe sometime my mom can come over, and you can show her how to bake one of these," Danny proclaimed, a ring of chocolate icing around his mouth. *Take that, Harold,* Alec thought.

After dinner Harold leaned in and lowered his voice so Alec's mother couldn't hear him. "Have you used the Ouija board again?" Alec shook his head, and Harold

32

laughed. "I guess it would be kinda weird if you had."

"Why are you even talking about it?" Danny put in. "You thought Alec was pushing it the whole time."

"I never said that!" Harold shot back, but he didn't look at Alec as he denied it.

"Here, look. Let's go upstairs," Danny said, "and we'll show you that thing I found."

Harold let the others lead him up the back stairs to the large attic room, but he shook his head when he saw the letters gouged into the windowsill. "You could have done that when you moved in," he said to Alec. "It's so dusty up here, we'd never know."

"Whatever, Harold," Danny said cheerfully, but Alec couldn't shrug it off so easily. *If you think I'm lying then why don't you just go home?*

"I think we should try the board again," Alec said. "This time *I'll* write down the letters."

They snuck the talking board up to his room and set it on his desk. Harold sat in the chair and Danny drew up another. Alec sat at the end of his bed with the notebook.

"Hello?" Danny said, and they waited. "Hello?"

"It's just what I thought." Harold took his fingers off the planchette and leaned back from the desk. "I *knew* you were pushing it."

Alec's heart knocked in his chest. "I wasn't!"

"Whatever." Harold rose from the desk. "Let's watch *Guardians of the Galaxy*."

Mrs. Frost made popcorn and brought it into the TV room, and if she noticed the silence that had fallen between the boys, she pretended not to. Alec, cheeks still burning with indignation, found himself wishing that Harold would fake a stomachache and go home. Some birthday this was turning into.

His mother said goodnight midway through the movie, and the house was perfectly still by the time the end credits came on. Alec switched off the television.

"I want to try the board one more time," he said. "Downstairs. Maybe it makes a difference. I'll take the notes."

Harold rolled his eyes, but Danny led the way into the dining room. They set themselves up as they had that first night, but Danny took the planchette and Alec the notepad. "Hello?" Danny said again.

This time the planchette sprang into motion, sliding toward the corner marked HELLO before spelling out

A-G-A-I-N S-P-I-R-I-T.

A pause, and then:

YOU HAVE NOT SUCCEEDED IN FRIGHTENING US
AWAY—

"Neither have you," Danny replied cheerfully. "I ain't afraid a' no ghosts!"

"I think we should test it," said Harold.

Danny frowned. "What do you mean?"

"We should ask it things no one else could know." Harold nodded at Alec. "Things *he* couldn't know."

"Don't be a doofus," Danny retorted. "You know he's not moving it. How could he be?"

MOTHER IS OUT PLANNING THE RALLY OR WE
WOULD NOT BE HERE—

At this Danny literally scratched his head. Alec found he could transcribe the words as the pointer completed them, that there was no need to write the letters down one at a time only to make sense of them afterward.

MRS GUBBINS SAYS YOU HAVENT BEEN BORN YET—

"Mrs. Gubbins?" Harold exclaimed. "What the . . . ?"

"Shhh! You'll wake up Alec's mom."

"Who is Mrs. Gubbins?" Alec asked.

MRS GUBBINS IS MY DOLL—A VERY SPECIAL DOLL—
SHE TELLS ME OTHER PEOPLES SECRETS—EVEN YOURS
SPIRIT—

"Don't call me 'spirit,'" he said when the pointer stopped. "I'm not a spirit. My name is Alec."

SEE JOSIE I TOLD YOU HE WAS A BOY—

Josie, Alec thought. *Short for Josephine.*

Harold leaned forward until his chin was almost on the board, as if he were about to whisper into the ear of someone invisible.

"Ask Mrs. Gubbins," he said, smirking. "What are Alec's secrets?"

MRS GUBBINS SAYS ALEC DOES NOT KEEP ANY
SECRETS WORTH TELLING—BUT YOU DO—

Danny laughed. "Very funny," Harold said sourly.

ONCE A LIAR ALWAYS A LIAR THATS WHAT MRS
GUBBINS SAYS—

Harold pulled away from the planchette and sat staring at the board, as if the invisible hand had reached up and slapped him. Danny eyed his friend, but did not remove his fingertips, so the pointer continued to dart between the letters.

CASSIE IF YOU INSIST UPON INSULTING THE SPIRITS
THEN DONT—

"Stop it," Harold said quietly, but Danny did not react.

"I said *stop it!*" With the back of his hand, Harold flung the pointer from the table, and it went sliding across the carpet before thudding loudly against the baseboard.

A moment later Alec heard a door open on the second floor, and his mother's footsteps come softly to the head of the stairs. She called his name, her voice thick with sleep. "Is everything all right?"

"Yes, Mom. Everything's fine. I'm sorry we woke you up."

"It's pretty late," she replied. "Aren't you guys tired yet?"

That was code for *Go to bed now, please.* Alec picked the pointer off the carpet—he was surprised it hadn't cracked—and put the board back in the drawer. Harold stared at the table, his arms tightly crossed. "Coming?" said Danny, and he nodded slightly. But when he and Alec went back into the family room and unrolled their sleeping bags, Harold did not follow.

A minute later the front door opened and closed, and when the boys went back to the front hallway they saw Harold's overnight bag was gone.

"That jerk," Danny said, shaking his head. "They really spooked him, didn't they? Oh well!" Alec lay awake, thinking not of that-jerk-Harold but of the portrait of Josephine Clifford his mother had placed on the mantel.

In the morning, Alec's mother insisted on calling Mrs. Yates to make sure Harold had gotten home safely. She turned away and lowered her voice as she spoke into the receiver. "The boys must have had some sort of a tiff last night . . . you're right, of course . . . they'll patch things up on Monday . . . and please tell him he's welcome to come back for pancakes and fruit salad."

"I've never seen him like that," Danny said as he poured the maple syrup. "He was like a totally different person last night."

"I don't know what I could've done differently." Alec pushed a piece of honeydew across his plate. "*I* didn't make the pointer move."

"Of course not." Last night's goings-on had not diminished Danny's appetite, and he tucked into his stack of pancakes with a cheerful face. "We gotta chalk it up as one of those things nobody's ever gonna be able to explain, like crop circles or Bigfoot. He'll get over it."

Somehow Alec doubted that. "Do you think we were really talking to somebody?"

"More than one somebody," Danny replied through a mouthful of pancake. "They were talking to each other, remember? And then there was that Mrs. Gubbins character. Nobody could've made that up." He took another bite and giggled with his mouth full. "*Mrs. Gubbins.* That's so ridiculous."

"They called each other by name," Alec said slowly. "First it was Josie, and then Cassie."

"So you've got two girl ghosts."

"What's that about ghosts?" said Mrs. Frost as she flipped another pancake on the skillet.

"We were telling ghost stories last night." Danny flashed Alec a conspiratorial look as he spooned out some fruit salad. "Wouldn't be a sleepover without 'em."

The phone rang, and when his mother answered it, Alec ran to the living-room mantelpiece and brought back the portrait of Josephine Clifford. "I think this is her," he said softly. "This is Josie."

Alec liked the way Danny looked at old photographs. He took a minute to *see* the person inside the photo—a person who, though dead and gone, had held as many hopes and dreams as the boys did now.

"If they lived here we should be able to find out about them," Alec went on. "The real estate agent told us a famous actress lived here once. Maybe she's one of them."

Danny looked up from Josie's face, and grinned. "I like the way you think, dude."

Votes for Women!
7.

Half of Edwardstown considered Lavinia Clifford a witch, a confidence artist, or both, while the other half quietly made and kept their appointments in her sumptuous reading room. No one doubted she was the little town's most prominent resident, though she rarely appeared in public.

In late October, however, the National Women's Committee invited "our esteemed Mrs. Clifford" to give the keynote speech at their autumn rally, and on this occasion even the most plainspoken skeptics treated her like a queen. The drunken men who inevitably loitered along the margins of these events could hardly summon a jeer between them. She was that magnificent.

Josie could not believe the woman who stood at

the podium was the mother who would not suffer a kiss upon the cheek, nor was she the mother who had humiliated her under the pretense of making her own mistakes. This was not even the mother who'd locked the study door to rehearse that selfsame speech well into the night.

There was a whiff of winter in the air, and the ladies in the crowd pulled their wool coats and furs snug around their necks as they lifted their faces to the stage beside the bandstand. "Our sisters in several of the western states have been given the right to vote, but what of the rest of us? Are we to sit politely by until we are too old to walk to the polls?" Lavinia Clifford's eyes shone, and her voice rang out like a victory bell. "Yes, the men who make the laws in Washington have asked us to wait. They say now is not the time, that we cannot press for our rights while the war in all its atrocity creeps across the European continent. They say it is only a matter of time before our nation is drawn into the conflict, and so we must wait.

"Wait? Pray, wait for what? If you would put us off for this war, you will certainly put us off for the next; for there *will* be a next war, and another. We women, the givers of life, know that war robs us of our sons, and the sons of those whom we would call our enemy, and that their sons are no less dear to them than ours are to us. We know, too, that the machines of war make other men wealthy beyond the grandest imaginings of we ordinary folk. We shall not believe what is convenient for them to tell us!

"Why, will our daughters be waiting, too? Our granddaughters? A century from now, will we still gather to demand our rights? I tell you, *we shall not wait!*"

As Josie listened, an unfamiliar feeling stole over her, something more complicated than excitement. The applause broke out—roaring and continuous, dotted with hoots and whistles from the otherwise lady-like—and it occurred to her that she was *proud* to be the daughter of the woman who stood on that stage beneath the red, white, and blue festoons, smiling serenely as the cheers went on and on.

The whole household had come out to the rally, and together they walked home from the park under a bright full moon. In between yawns, Cassie chattered about the women and their sashes and hats and their fancy words, and Emily's face glowed with the light of inspiration, and even Mrs. Pike and Mrs. Dowd went arm in arm like schoolgirls. As they opened the front door and filed inside, Josie listened to their laughter echoing in the cold, dark house. Mrs. Dowd lit the burner for cocoa, and Cass danced in anticipation while the milk warmed on the stove.

When the cocoa was ready, even Merritt accepted a mug, which he cradled between his broad white hands as if to warm them, though Josie noticed he did not take a drink. Her mother pointed to the high shelf where the spirits were kept, and Merritt rose, took down a bottle of whiskey, and poured a dollop into his mistress's cup.

The girls had only taken a few sips when Mrs. Clifford ordered them up to bed—the mother of the stage was well and truly gone now—and they scalded their throats trying to finish as much of the cocoa as they could. This had been the sort of evening that would not come again, and to have one's treat so rescinded merely confirmed it.

They changed into their nightgowns, weary limbs

still thrumming with the excitement of the rally, and raced into their tutor's room to vault themselves onto the bed. "My!" said Emily, who waited for them with a finger marking her place in *The Brown Fairy Book*. "This bed seems so much smaller than it was a moment ago." Cassie laughed as she propped Mrs. Gubbins atop the headboard. She laid her head in Emily's lap as Josie nestled herself beside them under the pinwheel quilt. Emily washed with lavender soap, and always smelled so sweet and grown up. She kept her toiletries in an elfin cupboard in the wall, and whenever she left it open Josie would marvel at the trappings of womanhood, the witch hazel and cold cream in glass bottles and the pearl-topped hatpins on the little velvet cushion.

Lately they'd been reading their way through *The Brown Fairy Book*. "The Enchanted Head" was the story Emily would read tonight, and she did the voices with great panache. It told of a man's head on a silver dish— still alive, mind—and how the man came to marry the sultan's daughter. "*I will never marry my daughter to such a monster!*" Emily roared, knowing it would thrill and frighten them in equal measure.

"*. . . When the merry-making was done, and the young couple were alone, the head suddenly disappeared, or, rather, a body was added to it, and one of the handsomest young men that ever was seen stood before the princess.*

'A wicked fairy enchanted me at my birth,' he said, 'and for the rest of the world I must always be a head only. But for you, and you only, I am a man like other men.'

'And that is all I care about,' said the princess."

"But why?" Cassie asked as Emily closed the book. "Why didn't the princess care? They couldn't ever go for a walk in the park. And she would have to feed him at every meal."

"I don't think the princess was concerned with having to spoon feed him. They had servants for that."

"But how could she be happy with a husband who hardly ever had a body?"

"I have an inkling." Emily smiled to herself as she laid the book on the bedside table. "Someday you'll understand."

Cassie pondered this. "Are you going to get married, Em?"

Their tutor gave her a sideways look. "Why, Cass! Are you trying to get rid of me?"

For a moment Cass mulled this over, and once she understood, she replied, "Oh, but why couldn't you and your husband go on living here with us?"

"I don't know that your mother would approve of such an arrangement."

"If Emily ever marries," Josie said, "she'll have to go to work for her husband instead, cooking his dinners and scrubbing the floors. That's what you do when you're married."

Cass frowned. "Did Mother ever cook dinners or scrub floors?"

Josie scoffed. "Hah! Never in her life."

"You're fortunate in that your family can afford to hire help," Emily said diplomatically.

"Then I'll have help, too," Cass declared. "I'll have a dozen butlers and a hundred maids because my husband will be the inventor of the . . . hmm . . . the sewing machine!"

"Somebody's already invented the sewing machine," said Josie, "and he's at least a hundred years old."

"Think of something that hasn't been invented yet," said Emily.

"But how can I do that if . . ." Josie loved to watch

her sister thinking hard about something. It was only a matter of time before she cracked the problem and a light came shining through. "I know! We could ask Alec! He's from the future, you know. Mrs. Gubbins says so. We can ask him anything we want."

"I'd rather he was a time traveler than a ghost, that's for certain." Emily regarded the little girl with sober curiosity. "What would you ask him?"

"Oh, anything. What I look like when I grow up, and what Josie looks like, and about the flying ships, and the name of the man I'm going to marry . . ."

With gentle fingers Emily brushed a lock of hair out of Cassie's eyes. "Do you think it would be good for you to know what's to come?"

"Of course it would! Then I wouldn't have to waste any time fretting about it. I could just sit back and look forward to it all."

"But what if he told you something that would make you unhappy? Or—consider this, little one—perhaps the act of him telling you would actually change what happens. It *could* change, if you were to know about it beforehand."

Cassie gazed up at her tutor with a conflicted countenance. Should she cling to what was comfortable to believe, or what might be nearer the truth?

"What if he told you," Emily went on, "that you were to marry a man named Maurice who worked in fertilizer, and you said to yourself, 'Oh *no*, I'd *never* marry a man who sells manure for a living,' so that when you met your Maurice, you spurned him without giving yourself the chance to fall madly in love. What then?"

"Don't toss him aside too soon, Cass," Josie said, mock serious. "Especially if his surname is Fitzmaurice.

There could be a lot of money in manure."

Cassie wrinkled her nose. "Maurice Fitzmaurice?"

Josie and Cassie dissolved into giggles, and Emily shushed them. "Or else we'll have Merritt knocking at the door. And I don't know about you girls, but I don't want to see what his face looks like in the dark."

"What of your parents, Em?" Josie rested her head on her elbow. "Were they very much in love?"

"I don't know. My mother passed away when I was three, and my father was in the Merchant Marine. I was lucky if I saw him once a year. I never felt as though I knew him well enough to ask those important questions."

"You always lived with your aunt and uncle?"

Emily nodded. "They have been as good to me as a mother and father could ever be. Someday you must come down to New York and meet them."

Cassie yawned. "I want to see a musical and go to the castle in the park and eat a strawberry ice cream in a hotel."

"Did you have any beaux when you lived in the city?"

Their tutor smiled. "A few."

"But why didn't you marry any of them?" Josie asked.

"They were nice enough young men. But I was on my way to college, and if I'd had any thoughts of marriage and children, I had to push them from my mind. You know, don't you girls, how important your education is? There was no question for me of giving it up." She paused. "More to the point, I did not love either of them." Their tutor played with the binding on her quilt, pensively running a finger along the old hand stitching. "You two are very fortunate. Your education will be provided for—perhaps you could go to Vassar, as I did, or to Smith or Wellesley—and when the time comes, you will begin your married life with an independent income. You will never want for anything."

In the blink of an eye their tutor had assumed the aura of a fortune-teller—much more authoritative than the mechanical soothsayer downstairs—and Josie felt a flicker of excitement in the pit of her stomach.

"Mother told you that?"

Emily nodded.

"I can have my twenty butlers, regardless," Cassie said with satisfaction. Then there came a peaceful silence, which the little girl ended by blurting out, "Mrs. Gubbins never married. She says she had heaps of beaux, and I asked her why she didn't marry any of them, and she said there was one she liked enough to marry, but whenever he came around to see her she couldn't stop sneezing."

"Stop talking nonsense," Josie sighed happily.

"I think it would be awful to have a husband who didn't agree with you," Cass went on.

"It was a good thing she didn't marry him, then," said Emily, with a twitching mouth.

"Mrs. Gubbins says I'm going to get married someday but Josie won't."

Josie sat up abruptly. There had been such a warm, contented feeling between them as they cuddled under Emily's quilt, and now it was gone.

Emily, too, was no longer smiling. "What could make you say a thing like that, Cassie?"

Cass shrugged. "I didn't say it. Mrs. Gubbins did."

"Oh, will you hush up about that silly old doll!" Josie cried. "Mrs. Gubbins doesn't say *anything*. She's only a toy."

"You're wrong," Cass said in a small voice.

"What if I said *you* were going to be an old maid? How would you like it?"

"I wouldn't. Because you'd only be saying it to spite me."

"Me, spite *you!*"

"Let it go," Emily broke in. "You said it yourself: she's talking nonsense."

The look on Cassie's face was as grave as if someone had died. It was this solemn attitude of *no one believes me* that pushed Josie to full-blown tears. She threw back the quilt and got to her feet, and did not turn when Emily called softly, "Josie, dear! Come and kiss me goodnight, at least."

She went into the nursery, burrowed under her quilts like a woodland animal in the dead of winter, and cried. Through her tears she was dimly aware of the murmuring going on behind the door, and she knew that Emily was gently—*too* gently!—admonishing Cassie for what she had said. Eventually the door opened and the light fall of little feet came slowly across the carpet.

"I'm sorry, Josie," Cassie whispered. "I didn't mean to hurt you."

Josie did not reply, not even when Cass reached out a finger and poked her through the blankets. She had spoiled this marvelous evening, and no apology could bring back that rare contentment. All the next day Josie spoke to her sister only when it was absolutely necessary, and did not look her in the eye even once.

Two days after the rally, the girls were seated at their school table, at work on their respective assignments while Emily sat by the window reading Upton Sinclair; rather, Josie was at work on her French composition while Cass drew a winged horse in her copybook. She kept turning the copy-book around and pushing it to Josie's side of the desk, and Josie would push it away again, ignoring Cassie's whispered pleas for her to admire what she'd made.

But Josie noticed when the little girl looked at her doll, which was propped up on the bookshelf, and paused as if she were listening. "Mrs. Gubbins says I shouldn't tell you everything she tells me. She says I hurt your feelings, but even so you're being terribly petty."

Josie sighed. "What did I tell you about *Mrs.-Gubbins*ing everything you say?"

"I don't know."

"Yes, you do. It's *supremely* irritating. If you think I'm being petty, then for heaven's sake, just say it."

"Does this mean you're not angry anymore?"

Josie tried to suppress a smile, and failed.

Seek and Ye Shall Find
8.

The boys did a Google search for "Clifford" and "Edwardstown, NY," and only two names showed up in the search results: William Clifford, mentioned as a businessman in New York City newspapers Alec had never heard of, and Lavinia Clifford, "The Edwardstown Sibyl."

"What's a sibyl?" Alec asked.

"It's like a fortune teller," Danny said. "But from a long time ago. Like ancient Greece."

The reading room of the Edwardstown public library had tall arched windows, geometric floor-tiles, and carved oak furniture, like a church of books. A red-haired woman, somewhere between college and his mom's age, was reading a newspaper behind the reference desk. She looked up as the boys approached the desk. "Hey there. How can I help you guys?"

"I just moved here," Alec began, "and we live in an old house, and the real estate agent said it was built by a famous actress. I think her last name may have been Clifford?"

"First name Lavinia, probably," Danny cut in.

The name tag pinned to the librarian's sweater read *Bernice*, and when she smiled at him encouragingly he felt a mild spell of shyness. "I was wondering . . . if you could tell me more about her?"

The librarian's eyes sparkled, as if she were about to let them in on yet another secret worth keeping. "You might say Lavinia Clifford was a *kind* of actress. She was a psychic medium back in the early twentieth century. She gave readings for people who'd lost their sons in World War I."

Alec and Danny traded a look. The talking board! It made perfect sense.

"You're very lucky to live in her house," Bernice was saying. "It's a wonderful piece of local history. It's on the corner of Sparrow and Hemlock, right?" Alec nodded, and Bernice rose from her chair and gestured for them to follow her. "Let's go back to the records room. I've got something you two will definitely be interested in."

Golden afternoon light spilled through the tall windows onto desks where people worked on laptops or leafed through the newspaper. She led them through an archway into a much smaller space with two long tables and three walls of gray archival boxes, all neatly labeled. No one else was there.

Bernice mounted a footstool to pull a carton off the top shelf. *LAVINIA CLIFFORD*, said the yellowed typewritten label. *1901–1927*. Danny lifted the lid and peered inside. "Wow!"

"Lots of goodies in there," Bernice said happily.

"Just be careful, okay? Some of this stuff is really fragile." Danny rolled his eyes as the librarian left the room, and Alec chuckled under his breath.

Inside the carton they found a stack of magazines, each of them individually sealed in clear plastic, and a scrapbook with an embossed leather cover bursting with newspaper clippings. There was also a small wooden recipe box, but when they opened it they found a collection of tiny black-and-white photographs sorted by tabs: *theater/early years; spirit photography; Henry Jennings; suffrage activities; Clifford family; testimonials.* This last section turned out to be portraits sent by grateful sitters—portraits, that is, of the deceased loved ones with whom they believed Lavinia Clifford had allowed them to communicate.

Danny spread out the stack of plastic-sealed magazines. "These are Spiritualist mags. I've seen them in my dad's shop. They're good for a laugh."

Alec chose the first magazine in the stack and gently pulled it out of the plastic. *The Night Side* was printed on the cover in bold, ornate type that looked a bit like the letters on the talking board. The table of contents included "Guidelines for the Construction of a Psychomanteum," "Some Verses Composed Through Automatic Writing," and "Fortune-Telling with an Ordinary Deck of Playing Cards."

"You think people actually took this stuff seriously?"

His friend shrugged as he flipped through the photograph file. "Lots of people did."

The magazine was falling apart, but Alec could tell it had been well produced, with detailed illustrations of the "ghost box," the various sectors of one's palm, and all that. It was too elaborate to be a joke.

Danny pulled out a small photograph of three girls

at a round metal table on a sunny terrace, the hedge—much lower then—curving around behind them. "Dude! That's your backyard!"

The oldest of the three wore a hat with a bunch of tiny flowers pinned on the side. She wasn't exactly pretty, but something in her face was tremendously appealing, as if she'd already decided to be your friend. The little girl, seated in the young woman's lap, had a mop of dark curls and a grin missing a few baby teeth—she had to be Cassie—and her older sister stood behind the chair with her hand on the woman's shoulder. Alec's eyes rested on Josie's face last. She was smiling only faintly, as if her thoughts were elsewhere.

"That's them," Danny murmured. "The girls we were talking to. This is so insane."

Alec turned back to the magazine and found what he was looking for at the bottom of the table of contents. "The Edwardstown Sibyl: A Profile of Mrs. Lavinia Clifford, Psychic Medium." A full-page portrait of Mrs. Clifford accompanied the article, and Alec kept glancing over at it as he read the opening paragraphs. The woman wore one of those old-fashioned puffed-up hairdos. She was beautiful by anyone's standards, with pale eyes, a long straight nose, and a slender neck. He had a feeling, though, that he might not find her so lovely in real life. There was something icy and untouchable about Mrs. Clifford—like she was only tolerating the mere mortals who took her photograph and copied down her words.

The boys began to read together. The article described Miss Lavinia Hare, a seventeen-year-old Broadway actress who, while playing a star in the sky, fell from her harness onto the stage thirty feet below. This, supposedly, was when the voices and visions began.

As the young actress recovered from her injuries, she began giving readings to all the stagehands and chorus girls of her company. When reporters arrived, she told them all about *their* dead relatives, too—and that's how she met her first patron, Horace Vandegrift, who owned a newspaper called the *New York Watchman*. She helped him find a lost family treasure, and her career was made.

Mr. Vandegrift took her on a European tour, and when she returned, Lavinia Hare became first Lavinia Malcolm, then Lavinia Clifford, though the article didn't say anything about her children. It did say, though, that when Mr. Vandegrift "passed into spirit himself" he left most of his money to Lavinia, and his "ne'er-do-well" nephew resorted to violence. Alec wondered at that. If she knew about things that hadn't happened yet, couldn't she have avoided it somehow?

The next part of the article was much more fun.

Visitors may encounter any one of four spirit controls, which speak through the medium during her trance state: Evenor, who purports to be a physician from the lost continent of Atlantis; Baldassare, a poet and alchemist of the Italian Renaissance; and Zazu, a Babylonian priest who perished in the fall of that once-great city, and has been known to lecture at length on the mystical benefits of volcanic mud baths. The fourth advisor has shown a curious reluctance to utter his name to anyone who has requested it, and declares that he has never experienced a human incarnation, though he will gladly play the piano for anyone who asks. Mrs. Clifford, it is worth noting, has never received any formal musical training.

The next part described a reading Mrs. Clifford gave for a young woman whose fiancé, a rock climber, was killed when his rope snapped during a sudden hailstorm. The author received a letter from the dead man's mother, who believed she had real proof of the medium's powers:

> The spirit of Mr. Vernon (channeled, of course, by Mrs. Clifford) mentioned by name a Mr. Frederick Barnett of Manor Hill, San Francisco, a friend of Mr. Vernon's who had accompanied him on his climbing expeditions to Inverness, Vancouver, and the "silver coast" of Argentina. Mrs. Clifford urged the ladies to warn Mr. Barnett of a man with two missing fingers on his right hand on an impending trip to Hidalgo, Mexico.

> Mr. Vernon's fiancé dutifully wrote to Mr. Barnett and apprised him of the warning, to which she received an understandably skeptical reply shortly before his departure. They later received a cable from Mr. Barnett in Tihuana, Mexico, informing them that he had been to a local tavern and encountered just such a man, who invited him to a game of cards. Minding the warning of his departed friend, Mr. Barnett quit the establishment immediately, and has lived to tell the tale.

> "I have never in all my days met a man who was missing his first and second fingers—or any fingers at all, for that matter," wrote Mrs. Vernon. "It is simply too unlikely a coincidence." We suspect that Mr. Barnett runs in considerably rougher circles than does Mrs. Vernon; but if it *is* a coincidence, it is a very curious one indeed.

"Coincidence, my butt," said Danny, and Alec agreed. If Josie could talk to them across a hundred years, then why couldn't her mother do all the fantastic things people claimed of her?

> It has recently come to the author's attention that Mrs. Clifford has agreed to a period of scientific study by Dr. Henry Jennings, head of the New York branch of the American Society for Psychical Research. The editors of *The Night Side* will eagerly await the results of this research, and will, of course, share those findings with our readership as soon as the good doctor has made them available.

Bernice appeared suddenly in the doorway, and both boys started in their chairs. "How you guys doing? You need any help?"

"We're okay, thanks," Danny said.

Alec, pencil in hand, noticed that Bernice was looking at his open notebook. "I love how stoked you are about living in Lavinia Clifford's house. Taking notes and everything!" The librarian smiled as she walked out again.

There was one more thing in the archive left to look at: a cache of letters inside a faded blue folio fastened with twine. Alec carefully undid the knot, and the boys flipped through the envelopes, all of which were addressed to Lavinia Clifford at 444 Sparrow Street, without the zip code. They opened a couple, but the letters were relatively short and not that interesting— the sender was just thanking Mrs. Clifford for putting them in touch with their dearly departed loved one, and explaining how much comfort it had given them.

But the last letter in the stack was not addressed to Lavinia Clifford, and it did not have a postage stamp. It was addressed, in the quaint penmanship of a century gone, to *Mr. Alec Frost.*

Alec stared at the envelope in his hand, his mouth hanging wide open. "Take it," Danny whispered. "Hide it in your notebook."

Alec shook his head. "Are you crazy?"

"Are *you* crazy? It's got your name on it!" Danny whisked the rest of the letters back into the folio, retied the knot, and hurriedly replaced the magazines and photograph file in the box. "Don't think about it as we're saying goodbye to Bernice, or it'll show on your face," Danny said under his breath. "Think about pizza or *Star Wars* or something."

The boys were on their way out of the library when Danny's cellphone buzzed, the word MOM flashing on the screen. Alec could hear Mrs. Penhallow's voice when Danny put the phone to his ear. "I think I had a son once. His name was Danny . . ."

"Aww, Mom! Can't I come home in an hour?"

"Nope. You promised your dad you'd dust the clocks this afternoon."

"Boo," Danny said as he ended the call. "Things were really getting interesting. I guess I can't make you promise to hold off reading it 'til I come back?"

Alec grinned. "Not a chance."

He closed his bedroom door and drew the folded pages out of the envelope. The paper was sturdy, but he was still a little afraid the pages would fall to dust between his fingers. The letter was dated November 3, 1915.

Dear Alec,

It is quite strange that I should be writing

to someone I have never met. But then, I never expected the talking board to live up to its name, so I suppose I must believe you when you tell me you have already read the letter I am about to write. The next time we communicate you must tell me the last number; we received 2, 0, and 1, but were interrupted before the pointer could settle on the final digit. Am I to understand that you live in the twenty-first century? Or are you a spirit playing a trick on me? I assure you I will not believe a thing simply because someone is determined to convince me!

I understand this is to be a one-way correspondence, which is a pity, as no one has ever sent me a letter. I must ask Emily to write me the next time she goes to New York, though of course she will be back again by the time I receive it.

I must tell you about Emily, who is our tutor. She lives with us and teaches me arithmetic, history, grammar and literature, Latin, and French, among other subjects. She is twenty-two years of age, and came to us soon after receiving her Bachelor of Arts from Vassar College. Emily is as dear to us as an older sister. Do you have any siblings, Alec? Cassie drives me to the brink at times with her instigating, but for the most part I am glad to be stuck with her. Now that I think of it, I suppose I am most content when we are at our school desk, and Cass is busy practicing her letters while Emily helps me to conjugate irregular verbs. Her room adjoins ours, and she reads aloud to us every evening. To my recollection that is something our mother has never done.

You have told me through the board that you

already know something of our mother. It is marvelous to think you have read about her at the public library! Mother has always sent away for our books, so I have only been to the library once or twice, but the next time I go there I shall think of you.

I am very curious to know the things you have learned about her. I cannot say I believe in her abilities, though, of course, I must acknowledge her skill at perceiving what a person most desires, and giving it to them through a sort of performance. You have told me she used to be an actress. I never knew this because Mother never speaks of the past. She must have her secrets, as I imagine all grown-ups do, but I do not think it is the secrets that have sealed her lips. Something terrible happened to her once, something I saw with my own eyes, but that is a subject for another letter.

Now that I know she once was an actress, of course, I cannot see how I never suspected as much. I can say she is a skilled performer because I sometimes hide myself in the back hall to hear all I can of her séances. Emily believes Mother truly does converse with spirits, or allows them to speak through her. I never argue too vehemently, for Emily is otherwise a very intelligent person, and I love her dearly.

Here is why I believe my mother is only a very skilled actress, and I write you this because you told me I should tell you this story. One day a young man walked by our house. He was running a stick along the slats in the fence, and he had a blue tabby-cat riding in the crook of his other arm. I was standing on the front walk, and when he reached the gate he turned, held up the puss, and declared, "Your mother can no more commune with the dead than this cat is the king of Norway." Once he had spoken, he disappeared around the corner of Hemlock Street.

I do not remember how I came to be outside on my own, as Mother has always been so careful to keep us in. This was the first time I heard anyone contradict the praise which came so frequently— that my mother was the greatest medium in the state of New York—and it set me thinking. Our fathers are dead and never return to comfort us through the lips of our mother. Why should everyone else's loved ones come back to offer words of solace, when ours do not?

A week later the blue tabby appeared on the back porch. It had no collar, and when it lingered I thought it might be a stray. I begged Mother to let us keep her, feeding the puss with milk and kitchen scraps over a period of three days while I wore her down, and she did eventually agree, however unwillingly. I named her Selkie and for weeks she slept with me, purring softly through the night.

The household staff—Merritt, my mother's guard, and Mrs. Dowd, the cook, and Mrs. Pike, the housekeeper—were none too kind to my little blue tabby. Once in the kitchen I even saw Mrs. Dowd kick her out of the way. In time we discovered Selkie was to have kittens, and Mother threw up her hands and said she never should have allowed "that furry demon" into the house in the first place. (Mind you, Selkie was always a gentle puss and had never done anything to warrant such slander.)

The kittens were born on the back porch, but before they could suckle Merritt dropped them one by one into a potato sack and brought them down to the rain barrel. I tugged on his arm, begging him not to do it, but it was no use. Mother told him to, of course. Merritt does not even put a morsel in his mouth unless she permits it.

I couldn't blame Selkie for distrusting me after that. She went away that night, and I did not see her again. I tell you this story so you understand why I sometimes feel, excepting the presence of Emily and my sister, as if this house is not truly my home. It is magical beyond words to think of you living here, too, in some happy time well into the future. When I think of it now, I feel as if I might belong here after all—you and me, both— provided, of course, that you are not some trickster of the ether.

Sincerely yours,
Josie Clifford

She'd signed her name with a flourish, as if the letter were intended for some important head of state. There was nothing to hear, yet the air hummed all around him. She might've written the letter in this very spot. Through the open door to the spare room he could see the locked cupboard—so that had been Emily's room, and his bedroom had belonged to the girls. The walls might have changed colors a dozen times, but it was the same room, the same window bench, the same leafy view over Sparrow Street. Alec could imagine the girl in the portrait moving through this room, reading and laughing and daydreaming, as if she'd only been here yesterday. A ghost can't write a letter, after all.

More Impossible Things
9.

Sometimes communion with the spirits left Mrs. Clifford thoroughly exhausted, and she took to her bed for two or three days. During these periods the entire household went into hibernation, even in the summertime. The cook did no cooking, and the household subsisted on whatever remained of meals served earlier in the week.

Josie reveled in these periods when her mother wasn't around to cast her disapproving glances (for it often seemed she cast no other kind); nor did the children care if they fed on bean stew or ham salad that had been sitting for two days in the icebox. These invalid days meant Emily and the girls could do as they liked—to go for longer walks by the river or up to the graveyard, have their lessons on the terrace, and best of all: to use the talking board. When Mrs. Clifford spent the day in bed, the servants went up to their attic rooms directly after supper, and there was no one to catch them in the reading room.

Emily, of course, made the most feeble of protests. "All right, then," she sighed. "But we mustn't make any noise."

Once again their tutor appointed herself secretary. Josie had become quite proficient at mentally stringing the letters into words while the pointer was still in motion, and she would announce the message to her companions. Cass laid the glass piece on the board and it took off, bound for HELLO, before any of them could even open their mouths to speak. Then it asked,

IS THIS JOSIE?

"How do you know my name?"

YOUR NAME IS JOSIE CLIFFORD—IVE SEEN YOUR
PICTURE—THEY FOUND IT IN THE WALLS—

"*My* picture? In the walls!? Are you the same sp—I mean, person we have spoken to twice before?"

The pointer moved to YES.

THERE WERE 3 OF US THE FIRST 2 TIMES WE
TALKED TO YOU—NOW ITS JUST ME AND DANNY—

"And you . . . you said your name is Alec?"

YES ITS ALEC—I LIVE HERE—

"Where is 'here'?" said Emily as she took down this line. "Do you mean to say you dwell in this house?"

Immediately the pointer moved to YES. Then it glided to the row of numbers, where it made a quick series of sidesteps on and off the number four. "Four,

63

four, four," Emily breathed. Then it moved, as they knew it would, to the letter S, then P, then A. *Sparrow.*

"But you can't live here!" Josie said. "That's *our* address."

"I *told* you," Cass whined. "I told you what Mrs. Gubbins said!"

Josie ignored her. "It doesn't make sense. The house was only built two years ago."

IT ISNT NEW WHEN IM LIVING IN IT—

Emily took a moment to make sense of these letters, then looked up at Josie, open mouthed.

DO YOU REMEMBER WHAT YOU TOLD US THE LAST TIME WE TALKED TO YOU—SOMETHING ABOUT MRS GUBBINS SAYING WE HADNT BEEN BORN YET?

"What is it?" the little girl said in a loud whisper. "What did they say?"

"They're reminding us of what you said the last time we used the board. You said Mrs. Gubbins said they hadn't been born yet."

"I *told* you, Josie! Why don't you ever listen to me?"

WELL, the planchette spelled out. I THINK SHES RIGHT—

"Mrs. Gubbins can't be right about anything, Alec, and I'll tell you why," Josie replied tartly—as if there *were* another person in the room with them, as real as Cass or Emily. "Mrs. Gubbins is only a doll." She paid no attention to the indignant look her little sister shot her across the board, and waited while the glass spelled out Alec's answer.

YOU SEE JOSIE—WE THOUGHT YOU WERE GHOSTS— WHO ELSE IS THERE TO TALK TO WITH A OUIJA BOARD?

"You didn't answer me the first time: how do you

know my name?"

YOUR NAME IS ON YOUR PORTRAIT—AND THEN YOU
WROTE ME A LETTER—I FOUND IT IN A BOX AT THE
LIBRARY—

"How could I have written you a letter? That's . . .
that's . . ."

IMPOSSIBLE? asked the pointer. I WOULDVE SAID SO
TOO—BUT ITS A REAL LETTER YOU ADDRESSED IT TO
ME AND ITS DATED NOVEMBER 3—1915—

Emily's eyes went wide. "Why, that's tomorrow!"

SEE? YOU HAVENT WRITTEN IT YET—

"You said you found it . . . in a library?"

IVE READ THINGS ABOUT YOUR MOM—I WENT
TO THE PUBLIC LIBRARY AND FOUND HER ARCHIVE
AND THERE WERE LETTERS AND ONE OF THEM WAS
ADDRESSED TO ME—

Emily frowned. "*Archive?*"

YOU TOLD ME ABOUT YOUR MOTHER—AND YOUR
SISTER—AND EMILY—their tutor gasped, half terrified
and half elated, as the pointer spelled out her name—
YOU TOLD ME ABOUT THE BOY WITH THE CAT—AND
WHAT HE SAID TO YOU ABOUT YOUR MOM NOT BEING
FOR REAL—AND LATER THE CAT CAME TO YOUR BACK
DOOR AND YOU KEPT HER FOR A LITTLE WHILE—YOU
NAMED HER SELKIE—

"How can you know these things? It's as if you've
reached into my head!"

"Shh," said Emily. "He's still talking."

—YOU DIDNT KNOW YOUR MOM WAS AN ACTRESS
SO I GUESS I SHOULD TELL YOU THAT TOO—WHEN SHE
WAS REALLY YOUNG LIKE 1-7—BEFORE SHE HAD HER

ACCIDENT AND GOT HER—UM—ABILITIES—

"Alec." Josie felt her pulse thudding in her fingertips. "You said you read about us in an archive. What is the year?"

Once more the pointer glided down to the row of numbers, and paused first on the two. Then it skipped over the one to stop on the zero. "I don't believe it!" Emily breathed. Then it slid sideways. Two, zero, one. Again it pulled up over the row of numbers, and skimmed along above them.

The hall door creaked open, and the girls sprang back from the talking board. They watched as a set of long white fingers curled around and gripped the jamb, and they heard Merritt's toneless voice before they saw his face. "What are you doing in here?"

The man stood staring at them with his glassy eyes. Josie glanced at the board and found the pointer motionless above the line of numbers. "This room is for your mother's use only," said Merritt. "You ought to have known better, Miss Jasper."

Emily swallowed hard and rose from the table. "My apologies, sir. It will not happen again."

He watched as Emily conveyed the board back to its drawer, with Cass on her heels proffering the glass piece with both hands. Josie, meanwhile, hid the notebook and pencil in her pocket. Merritt followed them upstairs and waited in the darkness until they were inside the nursery. Then they heard his slow and steady footsteps recede down the corridor, where he would resume his watch by Mrs. Clifford's bedside.

"He never ever sleeps," Cassie said as they unbuttoned their pinafores. "Mrs. Gubbins says so."

The Name on the Stone
10.

A little lane to the side of Danny's house led up to the graveyard, which was so old that no one living could remember anyone buried there. When Danny invited Alec, Harold, and the Wexler twins over to watch *Nightmare on Elm Street* on Halloween, there wasn't a doubt in anyone's head as to where the boys would end up that evening.

They decided they were too old for trick-or-treating, so Mrs. Penhallow brought out a glass punch bowl full of Snickers bars and Reese's Pieces along with a box of Thin Mints. Once the lights were off, the movie on, and Mrs. Penhallow distracted by the ringing doorbell, the Wexler twins brought out their grandfather's stash of souvenir whiskey bottles. Danny just rolled his eyes.

"Liquor is for losers," Harold sniffed, and the twins didn't argue, to Alec's relief. The bottles were the size of his mother's nail polish and looked just as unappetizing.

Harold turned to Alec. "Danny says you're still using the board."

Josh Wexler piped up before Alec could respond. "What board? You mean like a Ouija board?"

"He found an old one in his house. We had some . . . *interesting* results." Harold smiled slyly, as if he were about to tell a joke at Alec's expense.

"Like what?" cried the Wexler twins. "Tell us! Did you talk to any dead people?"

"Dead girls," Harold said with satisfaction. "Three of them."

Alec looked to Danny—*you didn't tell him about the letter, did you?*—but Danny was rummaging through a box of old DVDs.

"That's awesome!" Sam cried. "What did they say?"

"Were they murdered?" Josh asked. "Like, what if there was an Edwardstown serial killer?"

"Are we going to watch this movie, or what?" said Danny, and for a time the boys settled down in front of the TV. But all those chocolate bars and talk of Ouija boards had made them restless, and they only laughed at the scenes in *Nightmare on Elm Street* that were supposed to be scary. They put on their hoodies as Danny told his mom they were off to the Wexlers' for a new DVD.

The evening was just right for the holiday, the dark clouds holding an empty threat of rain. The cemetery's front gate wore a padlock so old that the chain wound around the wrought-iron slats was rusted through. The words inside the arch above the old gate read *MOUNT HOPE CEMETERY,* and in smaller letters beneath, *est'd 1797.*

68

One by one the boys hopped over the crumbling stone wall beside the gate. The tombs studding the hill were silhouetted against the dirty purple sky, the ground soggy and thickly carpeted with leaves. When the wind turned, Alec caught a whiff of something unpleasant— something rotting.

An owl hooted from high up in a sycamore. "Hey, Alec," Harold called. "Don't you have a date tonight?"

"A date? With who?" asked the Wexler twins in unison.

"With his dead girlfriend, of course."

"Shut up, Harold," Danny shouted back.

"Come on, let's go find her. She's got to be around here someplace." Harold took off up the hill, using his iPhone flashlight on the tilted headstones ahead of him. The Wexlers went after him, asking what name they should be looking for, but Alec didn't catch Harold's answer.

"Don't pay any attention to him," Danny said as they walked side by side through the wet grass.

"He's kind of hard to ignore." Alec sighed. "Sometimes I really don't get it, Danny."

"What do you mean?"

"Why you and Harold are even friends."

Danny didn't answer, and Alec was afraid he'd said too much. He turned to the right for a closer look at a mourning figure several paces down the row, and his friend did not follow.

The stone maiden regarded him sorrowfully, and he thought of the last time they'd used the board. No sooner were the words "twenty-fifteen" out of his mouth when he remembered the letter. Sure enough, the pointer had not moved again.

There came a triumphant shout from higher up the

hill. "Hey, look! I found her!"

Alec's feet carried him through the tall grass up the hill to the place where Harold was aiming the flashlight on his phone. *It can't be! I never showed him her portrait. He doesn't know her name.*

It was a squat white stone, mottled with green and brown mold, and a dense thorny bush grew up from behind as if to swallow it. There was no first name on the stone, no dates of birth or death, only the one name:

CLIFFORD

It was small enough to mark the grave of a child. "Hope you brought your shovel!" Harold cried gleefully.

At first Alec was too startled to react. Danny was the only one who knew who the "spirits" were. Finally he opened his mouth, wanting to say something that would sting in return—but he hadn't been quick enough, and what was the point? So he turned and made his way down the grassy slope, weaving between the crumbling headstones, and hurried past Danny without looking at him. "Hey, wait! Where you going?"

The clouds were clearing now, and the moon appeared—no longer full, but bright enough. The light made Alec's escape much easier than the climb had been. A shadowy figure loomed by the front gate, but, a moment later, he saw it was only one of the Wexlers, struggling to twist the cap off one of the souvenir whiskey bottles. He hardly looked up as Alec vaulted himself over the crumbling stone wall and set off down the road.

"Alec!" Danny shouted from up the hill. "Alec, wait!"

As Alec ran, a horrible too-familiar feeling swept over him, hot and sour and squirming. *He's only asking me to wait because he doesn't want his mother to find out we've been here. He couldn't keep the secret, and he doesn't even know I know.* He wanted to be alone, to hide someplace where no one else could lie to him.

Mount Hope, Reprised
11.

Josie loved to wander among the headstones as the sun slowly withdrew its light, making her way to the section where Mr. Clifford and her father were buried to lay a fistful of violets at the base of each headstone. It was strange to think of their fathers asleep forever just a few yards apart. Josie had read enough romances to know that when two men have loved the same woman they can never be friends.

Her father's stone was much smaller and plainer than Mr. Clifford's; his marker merely said DAVID MALCOLM, 1874-1904. Mr. Clifford's stone had an angel weeping over it, and a line from scripture: *In the twinkling of an eye, at the last trump: the dead shall be raised, and we shall all be changed.*

Mr. Berringsley had built a mausoleum for his parents at the top of the hill. They'd died when he was very young, but he'd had their remains moved here. It looked like a tiny gray temple, and you could stand at the wrought-iron gate and admire a three-paneled window of Tiffany glass, a sunrise in cream and gold beyond a ring of mountains and a tranquil blue lake, and a vale of irises in the foreground. There were names etched on the marble walls, those of Mr. Berringsley's parents as well as his sister's and his own. It seemed wrong to mark a tomb with the names of people who would live on for many years.

A rust-spotted moth flitted to and fro in the cold air, and Cass laughed as she darted between the stones in pursuit of it. She propped Mrs. Gubbins atop one of the markers and ran downhill again, so that the doll appeared to be keeping an eye on its owner.

Josie stood near the Berringsley mausoleum, watching her sister amuse herself. Emily came over to join her. "I've been thinking," her tutor said.

"What of?"

"The boy and the talking board." Emily smiled absentmindedly as the little girl reached out in vain to capture the moth, but her eyes were troubled. "Doesn't it give you the shivers? He could be standing on one of our graves *at this very moment.*" She paused to reconsider this remark. "At some point in the future, that is. Perhaps he's already been there, and he's too polite to say so."

Josie sat down on a mottled gray headstone with a sigh. "I suppose I hadn't wanted to think of that part." That morning she had written a rather long letter, telling the boy—or man? He might very well be grown, she would have to ask him his age—about Cass and Emily and her mother, and of the blue tabby cat she had loved and lost. But she had no idea where to put the letter so he would receive it.

Cass scooped up her doll and came trotting over. "Mrs. Gubbins says when you're dead long enough your headstone falls over and nobody remembers you anymore," she said breathlessly. "Only it doesn't matter then, because everyone else is dead too."

"Don't be morbid, dear," Emily said lightly. She took Cassie's hand and gazed at the doll cradled in the crook of the little girl's arm. "I wonder—how old *is* Mrs. Gubbins?"

"I don't know. I never asked her." Cassie turned to the doll. "How old *are* you, Mrs. Gubbins?" She paused, as if listening to the answer. "She says she's so old she's lost count."

"I believe it," Emily replied, and Josie laughed. Cass let go of her tutor's hand and ran up to the Berringsley mausoleum, where she sat herself on the steps and went on chattering away to her raggedy old plaything.

"I've been thinking, too, of our conversation the night of the rally," Emily went on. "Do you intend to ask him?"

"About what will happen to us?" Emily nodded. "I don't know," Josie said slowly. "Couldn't I ask for only the happy parts?"

"But what if knowing about the blessings could jeopardize their coming into existence? Perhaps it's like 'The Boy Who Kept a Secret.' If the boy had told his mother he'd dreamed he was king of Hungary, then he never would have been."

"You're thinking too much."

"Better than thinking too little," her tutor retorted, though not unkindly.

"If you believe the future is fixed," said Josie, "then there's no fear of knowing, is there?"

Emily sighed. "All I know for certain is that I'm frightened by all this. I don't want you girls getting mixed up in something you'll never be free of."

Josie looked up at her tutor, the hope and yearning plain on her face. "I don't want to be afraid. I don't want to run and hide whenever I meet a thing I can't understand. And I think . . ." She hesitated. "I think there must be a reason why he's permitted to speak to us."

Emily regarded her tenderly. "I won't ask you to promise you won't use the board unless I'm with you, for I know that's the sort of promise you're bound to break." Josie suppressed a smile. "All I ask," Emily went on, "is that you use your good sense. For heaven's sake, Josie, *be careful*. And don't deceive your mother. If she ever asks if you've used the board, you must come clean at once."

Josie considered this speech as she took her tutor's hand and went down the hill in the early twilight. Emily was right, of course. There was far more reason to fear the living.

Bygones
12.

The next morning Alec could only manage a couple bites of the pumpkin pie pancakes his mother made for him. He had no friends at all. No friends. *None.*

He could tell his mother wanted to ask, to fix whatever had gone wrong, but there was no making this right. There was a tiny grave in the cemetery with Josie Clifford's name on it, and if Danny had been a true friend Alec would never have known it was there.

It was November now, gray and gloomy—destined to be the sort of day with no satisfaction in it whatsoever. Alec sat on his window seat overlooking the big maple tree in the front yard, all the leaves now a vivid yellow, and his stomach turned over as he watched Danny round the corner and hurry up the front walk. The doorbell rang a moment later. *Don't let him in,* he wanted to shout, but then he'd have to explain himself, wouldn't he?

Alec heard his mother open the front door and welcome Danny inside, and then Danny's footsteps thundering up the front stairs. The knock at his bedroom door was loud and elaborate, like a passcode for a secret society they hadn't invented yet.

"Go *away*," Alec said. He wished he could lock the door, but that key was missing too.

The knock came again, aggravatingly cheerful. A minute later Alec heard a jangling sound and a bunch of metallic things spilling onto the hallway carpet, then the creak of the spare-room door. Alec went to the adjoining door and opened it. Danny stood in front of the locked cupboard with two fistfuls of antique keys— just the kind that might finally unlock that little door.

He turned to Alec and grinned. "Are you going to help me open this thing or what?"

Alec folded his arms. "You can't just come right in like you live here and act like everything's okay."

Danny sighed as he plopped himself down on the floor. "I'm sorry. I'm really sorry, Alec. I thought if I told Harold about the letter that he'd *have* to believe us. I never thought he'd be such a jerk about it." Alec shot him a look: *I could have TOLD you that would happen.*

"I know, I know," Danny said. "It was stupid, and I'm sorry, and I was up all night trying to think of a way to make it up to you."

Alec scoffed. "*All* night, huh?"

"Well, it didn't take me that long to remember my dad's stash of keys," Danny answered earnestly. "But I was wide awake feeling guilty until at *least* two."

Something occurred to Alec then, as he sat down beside his friend and began lining up the old keys along one of the planks of the hardwood floor: Danny had messed up, but he hadn't done any harm. When had his father ever apologized for ruining what had always felt like a happy family? He hadn't yet, and maybe he never would. Alec glanced up at Danny and felt a swell of something nice in his chest—a mixture of affection and relief.

Danny finished arranging the keys and handed the first to Alec. "Let's switch off," Alec said as he slid the tip of the key into the hole. "Wouldn't it be awesome if one of these keys worked?"

But it didn't fit. Danny tried the second key, and the fourth, and the sixth. He'd brought more than three dozen keys, but it didn't take them long to try them all. Most didn't fit into the keyhole, and the few that did fit refused to turn.

"That's the last one," Danny sighed as Alec began scooping up the keys to return to the antiques shop. "Now we've tried every stinkin' key in town."

"Is it possible this lock can only have one key?" Alec asked. If that were true they'd never be able to open it.

"Dunno. I'll ask my dad."

The boys launched themselves onto the spare room bed and regarded the little wooden door in the wall. "I wish I had X-ray vision," Alec said. There was no *way* that cupboard was empty.

The Times Machine
13.

Merritt must have told their mother he'd found them using the board, yet she'd said nothing of it, and for days Josie mulled over what this might mean. It was impossible she'd changed her mind and given them permission, for she'd driven them out of the reading room a hundred times and would have been furious had she ever discovered Josie hiding in the back hall. No, Mrs. Clifford was likely waiting to catch them at it a second time, at which point she would deliver her punishment with even greater satisfaction.

Josie understood that her tutor could not be found using the board again. What if Emily were to lose her position? But she didn't see why she couldn't use the board on her own, so long as Emily knew nothing about it.

One night in the middle of November, Emily read them "The Green Knight" out of *The Violet Fairy Book* before sending the girls to bed. Josie waited until Cassie's breathing grew slow and even before tiptoeing out of bed with her notebook and blanket.

She ventured into the reading room, switched on the electric lamp, laid the rolled-up blanket at the foot of the door to block the light, and pulled out the talking board. "Alec?" she whispered. "Are you there?" The glass piece moved to HELLO, then spelled out her name.

YOU LEFT SUDDENLY LAST TIME—DID YOU GET IN TROUBLE?

"Merritt found us and we had to put away the board. I told you about Merritt in the letter, didn't I? I wrote it the day after you told us about it."

YOU TOLD ME A LITTLE—HES YOUR MOTHERS BODYGUARD?

"Yes. He's a very strange man. The kind of person who makes the gooseflesh rise up and down your arms whenever he comes into the room."

HES PROBABLY GOOD AT HIS JOB THEN ISNT HE?

"I suppose he is." She sighed. "Emily can't use the board with me again. I couldn't bear the thought of my mother sending her away. Oh, there are so many things I wish to ask you, Alec! I have so many questions! How am I to know beyond all doubt that you're speaking to me from the future? How will I know for certain this is not a trick?"

IF ITS A TRICK THEN SOMEBODYS PLAYING IT ON ME TOO—HAVE YOU PUT THE LETTER IN THE FILE YET?

"I haven't yet, no. I'm not permitted to go into Mother's study."

OH WELL—I GUESS YOU HAVE PLENTY OF TIME—
YOULL FIGURE OUT A WAY OR ELSE I WOULDNT HAVE
FOUND IT—

She mulled this over. Of course Alec was right. It was as if there were a secret equilibrium which governed all the universe, and which every living creature must do their part to preserve.

I WISH I COULD SHOW YOU ALL THE THINGS IVE
FOUND—THE NEWSPAPER AND MAGAZINE ARTICLES
ABOUT YOUR MOTHER—THE OLD PICTURES OF YOU AND
YOUR FAMILY—THE LETTERS FROM ALL THE PEOPLE
WHO WENT TO SEE HER—

Her own experience supported what he was telling her. Her mother received so many letters from grateful one-time clients that Josie could never remember a time when she'd actually responded.

I KNOW YOUVE PROBABLY SEEN ALL THAT STUFF
YOURSELF—BUT IF YOU COULD SEE HOW OLD EVERY-
THING IS—THESE PAPERS HAVE BEEN SITTING IN A BOX
FOR I-0-0 YEARS—

A hundred years! It was beyond imagining, like setting out for the moon on foot.

THERES SOMETHING ELSE TOO—DANNY AND I
WERE UP IN THE ATTIC AND FOUND WORDS SCRATCHED
INTO THE WINDOWSILL—IT SAID HELLO ALEC—

"Your name, scratched into the attic windowsill! Who could have done that?"

YOU—MAYBE?

"Why, when I could say hello to you right now?" she laughed. "How about this. You say you have access to archives. Is the *New York Times* still printing?" The pointer moved to YES. "Could you read the front page—say, two weeks from now?"

SURE—I CAN DO THAT—

"Today's date is November 14th, 1915, so perhaps you could look for the newspaper from the 28th. The next time we speak, tell me what each of the front-page headlines will be. If I find all that you have told me on the morning of the 28th, then I shall be convinced."

THATS A GOOD IDEA JOSIE—I CAN DO IT RIGHT
NOW—HOLD ON A SEC—

For two minutes she waited with the fingers of one hand resting on the pointer, the other tightly grasping her pencil. How could he recover a century-old newspaper in the middle of the night?

FOUND IT—HERE GOES—GREECE DELAYS PLEDGE
TO THE ALLIES WHO NOW HAVE LANDED 125000
MEN—SERBS ADVANCING RETAKE KRUSHEVO—KITCH-
ENER ARRANGES FOR MORE AID BY ITALY—LONDON
WILL ACCEPT NEW TEMPERANCE LAW—SUBMISSION
TO DRASTIC ORDER SIGNIFICANT OF THE WAR SPIRIT
NOW PREVAILING—OH HERES A GOOD ONE—HE FELL
10000 FEET AND LANDED SAFELY—COLONEL MAITLAND
PROVED HIS AEROPLANE PARACHUTES EFFICACY IN HIS
OWN PERSON—

"Ten thousand feet!" she breathed. "How could you find the newspaper so quickly?"

ITS CALLED THE TIMES MACHINE—ON AN IPAD—A
SORT OF COMPUTER—I KNOW THOSE WORDS DONT

MEAN ANYTHING TO YOU—SORRY ITS HARD TO
EXPLAIN—

"Please try!"

IMAGINE YOU COULD READ ANY NEWSPAPER FROM
ANYWHERE IN THE WORLD—FROM ANY DATE—YOU
CAN DO A SEARCH FOR IT AND IT SHOWS UP ON THE
SCREEN—

"Screen?"

LIKE A BLANK PAGE THAT FILLS UP WITH WHAT-
EVER YOU WANT TO LOOK AT—

"Magic," she murmured, and when the pointer spun
she knew he was laughing.

ITS JUST TECHNOLOGY—

"Well, in the meantime we may as well speak as if
all this is true."

IF YOU COULD SEE THESE THINGS YOUD KNOW
NO ONE COULD HAVE INVENTED IT ALL JUST FOR A
LAUGH—I KNOW YOU DONT REALLY BELIEVE YOUR
MOTHER IS PSYCHIC—

"I did write you that, didn't I?" Swiftly the pointer
headed for YES.

BUT IF YOUR MOTHER WAS CHEATING DONT YOU
THINK YOUD HAVE CAUGHT HER?

This was the troubling part of Josie's conviction.
The children of other so-called mediums concealed
themselves in spirit boxes and under tables, appearing
as wraiths or glowing hands at the very moment their
gullible sitters were expecting it. Lavinia Clifford could
have easily used her own children to perpetrate her
fraud, but she had never done so. Josie admitted this to

her friend, who replied: THEN YOU CANT SAY FOR SURE
SHES FAKING IT CAN YOU?

She rolled her eyes at the empty room. "I suppose
not."

IT MUST BE WEIRD—ALL THOSE SAD PEOPLE
COMING IN AND OUT ALL THE TIME—AND YOUR MOM
SAYING SHE GETS TAKEN OVER BY SOME DUDE FROM A
LOST CONTINENT—

Dude. What a funny word. "It isn't strange when
we've always lived this way."

I GUESS ITS THE SAME AS DANNY ASKING IF
ITS WEIRD THAT I HAVENT SEEN MY DAD IN TWO
MONTHS—

"Oh," she said. "Your friend Danny, he isn't with
you?"

The pointer moved to NO.

"Is he a friend from school?" Then she reminded
herself that Alec might be a good deal older than she
imagined. "You *are* in school, aren't you?"

YUP I AM—HE SAYS HIS MOM ALWAYS MAKES HIM
GO HOME JUST WHEN THE REALLY INTERESTING STUFF
STARTS TO HAPPEN—

"Tell me about your life, Alec. The future is much
more interesting than the present."

I FEEL THE SAME WAY ABOUT THE PAST—

"Nonsense," she laughed. "Now, what is the year,
exactly?"

2-0-1-5—

"Marvelous!" she whispered. "A century, precisely!"

YOU KNOW WHATS FUNNY JOSIE—WE ARE 100

YEARS APART BUT NOT EXACTLY—YOU SAID ITS
NOVEMBER 14 BUT ITS STILL THE BEGINNING OF
NOVEMBER HERE—WHEN 2 PEOPLE ARE TALKING ON A
COMPUTER BUT THERE ARE A FEW SECONDS BETWEEN
SENDING AND RECEIVING SOMETHING ITS CALLED A
LAG—THIS IS THE LONGEST LAG EVER—

"You must tell me *everything*. Have you been to
Mars? Do you have your own airship?"

The pointer began to whirl. Josie frowned. "Why are
you laughing? We have aeroplanes in 1915, you know. It
isn't a silly question."

YES OF COURSE WE HAVE AIRPLANES—LIKE THE
WRIGHT BROTHERS RIGHT?—BUT ONLY VERY RICH
PEOPLE HAVE THEIR OWN AND THEY DONT USUALLY FLY
THE PLANES THEMSELVES—

"How long would it take you to get to London?"

ABOUT 6 HOURS—

"Six *hours*! Then I suppose you go to Europe all the
time!" She heaved a sigh of envy. "Before we were born
Mother traveled to all the great cities—London, Paris,
Rome, Vienna—but we've never been."

WE WENT TO SCOTLAND LAST YEAR BUT WE DONT
GO ALL THE TIME—PLANE TRIPS ARE EXPENSIVE AND
MY DAD CANT TAKE THE TIME OFF WORK—HES A
LAWYER—

"Ah, yes. I imagine he must work long hours." Then
another question occurred to her. "How old are you,
Alec?"

The pointer moved down to the numbers. One, two.
"Me too! I'm almost twelve!"

WHEN IS YOUR BIRTHDAY?

"The 26th of January."

THEN IM OLDER THAN YOU ARE—

"*Older!* How do you reckon?"

YOU JUST SAID YOU WONT BE 1-2 TIL JANUARY AND
IM ALREADY 1-2—

"And *I* was born in 1904!"

ALL RIGHT—ALL RIGHT—YOU WIN—

Then Josie laughed, too, and the pointer spun on both ends. But her heart gave a nasty thud as she strung together the message that came next:

ALEC WHAT ARE YOU DOING SWEETS—I HAVE TO
GO—

"Oh," she said. "Well, goodnight then, Alec."

It was clear the first part of the message had come from someone else—his mother, she supposed—and that there was no point waiting for the glass to move again.

Tell Me Everything
14.

"Alec? What are you doing, sweets?" His mother was standing in the doorway, squinting against the light from the chandelier.

"I have to go," he whispered, and straightened up to face her. "Nothing—I'm just—"

"Who are you talking to?" His mom came into the room, hugging herself in her oversized cardigan, and stared down at the talking board on the dining table. "Is that . . . a Ouija board? Where did you get that?"

He pointed to the massive mahogany cabinet, where he'd left the drawer a few inches ajar. "It came with the house."

Alec watched the fog of sleep receding. Her eyes grew bright, and he could almost see the gears clicking into motion inside her brain. "You found this, and you never told me?"

"I was going to! It just seemed like such a neat little secret that . . . that . . . I wanted to keep it for a little while."

"A secret, huh?" She folded her arms. "You were playing with this when Danny and Harold stayed over, weren't you?"

He nodded, his eyes on the table. He didn't want to talk about Harold, and he *certainly* didn't want to tell her what was happening with the board.

"Why are you being so secretive, Alec? You've never kept things from me before."

"I don't mean to be," he said in a small voice. "I never meant to keep it from you." *I only hid it because you wouldn't believe me if I told you everything.*

She sighed. "Put it away and get up to bed. You can use it, but not too often, and not this late at night. Okay?"

When Alec came down for breakfast the next morning he knew by the way his mother stirred the oatmeal that he was in for a Talk. "I know it's been a rough few months," she began as she handed him a bowl. "It feels so weird for me to not be talking about your dad. It feels so wrong that it's just the two of us now."

He reached across the table and patted her hand. "I know, Mom."

She tried to smile. "And I can't talk to you about certain things," she went on, "because I want to do the right thing. I don't want to say anything I might regret." She took a slow sip of coffee, and it occurred to him that this conversation wasn't any easier for her than it was for him. "Maybe that doesn't make sense to you right now, but I think it will someday. Your dad . . ."

She broke off and looked out the window, cradling her coffee mug with both hands, and her eyes were bright with tears. "Your dad . . . he hurt me very badly. It's the first time I'm saying that, but I haven't *had* to say it. I know you know."

Alec nodded.

"And you know why we're talking about it now, right?"

Suddenly he couldn't look her in the eye. "Because of last night?"

"Yes." She sighed. "More than anything else right now, I need you to be honest with me. Even when it's hard. *Especially* when it's hard. I *need* you to be straight with me, Alec, and not only because it's the right thing to do. Do you understand what I'm trying to say?"

He'd lied to her before, of course—that first time she tried to bake a vegan chocolate cake, the cake was dry and the icing was runny, but he told her it was delicious; or the time she wanted to wear an ugly orange blouse to his fourth-grade graduation ceremony and he told her she looked great—but this time was different. He had to tell her the truth, even if he got in trouble for it. Even if she thought he was insane.

Alec took a deep breath before he spoke. "What if I told you the truth, but it sounded totally impossible. Like I had to be making it up, even though I wasn't?"

She reached for his hand and squeezed it. "Tell me everything, and I promise I'll try my best to believe you."

Alec glanced through the living room doorway where Josie's portrait still sat looking out over the mantel. Mrs. Frost looked at him questioningly, and he hurried to retrieve the photo. He handed it to her, then ran up the back stairs to get Josie's letter from his desk.

Alec said nothing as he handed her the letter, and she said nothing as she looked at his name on the envelope. There was a strangely blank look on her face as she read the letter, and for once Alec had no idea how she might respond.

When she looked up from the page her eyes were troubled. "It's real," Alec said hurriedly. "It's a hundred years old. She's *alive*, and she's going to write me more letters and leave them in a place I haven't looked in yet . . ."

Mrs. Frost was shaking her head. "Alec . . ."

"Danny knows about it too! He's read the letter. We found it in the archive at the library. His dad can tell you that letter is really a hundred years old!"

She regarded him sadly. "I know, sweets. I can tell how old it is."

"Then *say* something, Mom. Tell me you believe me." *Tell me I'm not crazy*, he thought.

But she stared through the bottom of her mug and didn't answer.

"Can I still use the board?" he asked in a small voice. *Please, please, please say yes!*

His mother shook her head, and let the letter fall softly to the table as if it contained bad news. "I . . . I don't think . . ." She drew a deep breath. "I need to think about this. Can you give me some time?"

Alec nodded, avoiding her eye as he slid the letter back into the envelope. *What was there to think about?*

A Miserable Feast
15.

The week before Thanksgiving Mrs. Clifford announced at breakfast that they would be entertaining a scientist. "What sort of scientist?" Josie asked.

"His name is Dr. Henry Jennings, and he will be here to study me over a period of months," their mother said as she sipped her tea. "A thorough investigation, he calls it. He is a psychical researcher from the city, and when he is here he will stay at the hotel."

"Why is he studying you, Mama?" Cass asked. "Is it so no one can call you a phony ever again?"

"Where did you hear that word?" Mrs. Clifford looked at Emily and raised an eyebrow, as if the schoolroom were the only place it was possible to learn anything. "It is a nasty little slang word, Cassandra. You must not use it again."

Dr. Jennings was the tallest man Josie had ever seen apart from Merritt, and broad too, with a neatly trimmed black beard, ruddy cheeks, and a striding carriage that reminded her of a lumberjack in a storybook. He was a very learned man though, with an English accent that occasionally sent Cassie into wildly inappropriate fits of giggling during his introductory visit.

It was decided that Dr. Jennings would conduct his first experiment the following day, and Josie had no intention of keeping to the nursery. Emily relented only when Josie promised to spend her afternoon free time on an additional history composition. "You do know, don't you, that I have utterly failed you on the matter of discipline?" she sighed. "Heaven help me if she catches you."

Josie waited on the back stairs while Mrs. Pike shut out the daylight. Then she crept down the darkened hallway and knelt at the reading-room keyhole. The doorbell rang and the housekeeper showed the doctor and his secretary into the room. Clad in gray silk, the secretary—the doctor called her Miss Whipple—carried a small leather briefcase, which she opened on the reading table. When Mrs. Clifford entered, the doctor explained that they must have natural light, for it was the secretary's job to transcribe all that was said during the session—that is, if Mrs. Clifford had no objections?

There was a slight pause. Under any other circumstances Josie knew her mother would not want such a definitive record of what she had or hadn't said, in case the sitter ever used it against her, and the lantern-light added to "the effect." It would not do to refuse Dr.

Jennings, however.

"Of course," said Mrs. Clifford. "I have no objections."

Miss Whipple pushed back the curtains. It was odd to see the reading room in the afternoon light, so devoid of mystery.

"Let us begin," said the doctor. There was a brief silence, and, as usual, the air in the room grew heavy. "Is there an entity who has assumed command of Mrs. Clifford's physical body?" Dr. Jennings asked, and his secretary began to write quite rapidly.

"There is," Mrs. Clifford intoned.

"Please identify yourself."

"I am Baldassare, the poet of Volterra. It has been nearly four centuries since the end of my last incarnation on the Earth-plane."

"Ah! *Buongiorno, Signore*," the doctor replied jovially, and went on speaking in Italian for a short while. Josie listened with admiration.

The "poet" replied in English. "I have spoken through Mrs. Clifford many times, and will do so on many occasions in the future."

"Notice," said the doctor to his secretary, "that he will not reply in what he claims is his native language."

"I am well aware of your travels in Italy, Doctor," replied Mrs. Clifford with a sniff of disdain. "I know of your research in the Vatican library, and of the unfortunate theft in the Piazza San Marco . . . and of that charming *signorina* in Trieste." There followed an uncomfortable pause. Josie heard the doctor and his secretary shifting in their seats, and sensed that the "poet of Volterra" had taken Dr. Jennings down a peg. "I have no patience for such petty appraisals," Mrs. Clifford went on. "We shall converse in *your* native language."

"Very well, Signore. How many of you assume control of Mrs. Clifford's physical form?"

"We are four. The others will present themselves to you in due time."

"Why have you chosen to communicate through Mrs. Clifford? What is your purpose?"

"I, along with my cohorts, wish to raise the human race to a higher realm of spiritual consciousness. We hope to accomplish this by telling you of more advanced civilizations in other solar systems, and by proving to you the immortality of the soul."

"You say there is intelligent life elsewhere in the universe?"

Mrs. Clifford laughed the sort of laugh that otherwise never passes the lips of a lady. "You are a learned man, Dr. Jennings. I wish you would not ask me such questions. We have so little time, by your watch."

"On the contrary, Sir—I must ask these questions if I am to determine whether you are merely a subliminal portion of Mrs. Clifford's own personality."

"That, I fear, is the conclusion you will make regardless of what truths I describe to you."

"I see," the doctor replied. "Then I wonder if I might ask you a more practical question. Do you serve solely as Mrs. Clifford's spiritual conduit, or are you also responsible for her physical well being?"

"I understand your meaning. We did indeed warn her of the danger posed by Mark Vandegrift and his associates. It was her choice to remain vulnerable to his assaults." Lavinia Clifford lifted her chin, and even through the keyhole Josie could see her eyes were glassy and remote. "I know what else you wish to ask me, Doctor. I know that you will not believe what we say until we have proven the reach of our knowledge. And so now I shall tell you of other things in your own history."

Again the doctor adopted a cheery tone, though Josie could hear the falseness in it: "I wish you to reveal nothing that would surprise my mother."

"Your mother has been dead lo these ten years. She has known for quite some time of the things you kept hidden."

Dr. Jennings made a sound of amusement. "A man without a secret is a man who has not lived."

"On this we are agreed," said Mrs. Clifford with that odd masculine laugh. "You do know, don't you, Doctor, that it was my compatriots who arranged that you should come to Edwardstown to study Mrs. Clifford? I, on the other hand, had my reservations."

"And why is that?"

"You will not live long enough to complete this work, which would have cemented your reputation."

Her mother was fearless, Josie had to admit. First she had alluded to some possibly unsavory goings-on in Italy, and now she was predicting the doctor's premature demise!

"Weak heart," Dr. Jennings said dryly. "I have already outlived my father."

Mrs. Clifford nodded, slowly but emphatically. "You seek proof, and proof I shall give you. Then we must begin the work."

"What sort of proof?"

There was a long silence, the longest yet, and when Mrs. Clifford broke it she no longer spoke in a man's voice. "Viola. Viola is . . . here."

The air crackled with electricity. Josie put her knuckle between her teeth with suppressed excitement.

"Viola who?" the doctor asked sharply.

Mrs. Clifford's mouth twisted into a smirk. "You have known only one Viola."

"I presume I am no longer speaking with Baldassare, the poet of Volterra?"

"It is I, Lavinia Clifford, with Viola's lips at my ear."

"Tell me," the doctor demanded. "What does she say?"

"There was a row at her funeral, which you instigated. Something to do with a rival of yours. Things were said—mean things, petty things. It nearly came to fisticuffs. She was so disappointed, Henry."

"I don't see how she could be," he retorted. "She wasn't there."

"She never cared for him in that way. Viola loves you still, but she wishes you had not succumbed to your despair." The doctor made a noise in his throat, almost as if someone were strangling him. "You wore a gardenia in your buttonhole," Mrs. Clifford went on. "Clipped from the bush outside her mother's kitchen window."

"Flowers at a funeral, eh?"

"Her father . . . he did not come in time. You wrote him a letter, but he never received it. He blamed you for not coming to fetch him."

Another long pause. The doctor cleared his throat. "I think we have accomplished enough for one day."

"Interesting, isn't it, how 'feast' and 'fast' are only one letter apart," Emily remarked as the delectable odors of garlic, sage, and roasting turkey drifted up to the nursery. Mrs. Clifford had decreed there would be no holiday where their schooling was concerned, but

96

the girls knew this was only to keep them out of the servants' way as they prepared for company. Mr. Berringsley, his sister, and two friends were joining them for dinner at three o'clock. The cook had no time to fix them any luncheon.

"Breakfast feels like a hundred years ago," Cassie agreed. "Do you suppose I could go down and ask for a little something from Mrs. Dowd?"

The girls went down to the kitchen where Mrs. Dowd promptly shooed them off. So they returned to the school table, and for another two hours Cass went on complaining of her growling stomach. Finally Josie said, "For heaven's sake, either go down and ask again, or hush up about it."

Emily gave the little girl a sympathetic pat on the shoulder. "Perhaps by now she'll have everything well in hand, and will be more amenable to giving you a little something."

With a grin of anticipation Cassie slipped out of the room, returning several minutes later with telltale crumbs in the corners of her mouth. "What did she give you?" Josie whispered, but her sister gave her a queer look in place of an answer.

The afternoon wore on, and the scents wafting up from the kitchen continued to tantalize them. Josie completed her essay as Emily patiently listened to Cass read aloud from *The Centennial Children's Book*. "May I go down for a snack?" Josie asked.

Emily nodded and glanced at the clock. "There's only an hour until dinner. I think we've done enough studying for today." Cass whooped as she shut her reader with a *thump*, and Josie went down the kitchen stairs.

She found her mother consulting with the cook.

"Everything nearly ready, Mrs. Dowd?"

"All but the dessert, Mrs. Clifford. I'm afraid I must make another pudding."

"Why, what's wrong with the one you made this morning?"

"Someone's stuck her fingers in it, ma'am." Mrs. Dowd nodded to the bowl on the counter. "I left it in the pantry to set, and that's how I found it."

Mrs. Clifford lifted the cheesecloth to survey the damage. "The little beast!" she said under her breath. "You're right, Mrs. Dowd. We can't serve it."

"Couldn't you just trim off the damaged part, and put the rest in a smaller dish?"

Josie was rewarded for this suggestion with a scornful glance from her mother. "Go upstairs and find your sister," she said, and turned back to the cook, "Leave what's left of the pudding on the table. Do what you can, Mrs. Dowd—whatever dessert is quickest to make." Then she swept out of the kitchen under a black cloud.

Josie went slowly up the steps. She found Cassie and Emily in front of the vanity, where Em was doing the little girl's hair. She met her sister's eyes in the mirror and watched her face fall. "She wants you downstairs."

"Why?" Emily laid down the hairbrush and gently turned Cassie from the mirror. "What have you done?"

Cass tried to look away, but Emily lifted her chin with a finger. "There's no sense hiding from it, little one. Confess, and be on your merry way with a clear conscience."

"If only Mother were so forgiving," Josie sighed.

"I ate some of the pudding."

"Oh, *Cass*! Whatever possessed you to do such a thing?"

She pouted. "Breakfast was ages ago and that mean old Mrs. Dowd wouldn't give me even a tiny bite to tide me over." Emily was still regarding her with that sad, regretful look. "I couldn't help it," Cass went on in a small voice. "The pudding looked too good."

"Not anymore," said Josie.

Emily took Cassie's hand and led her downstairs. "Well, if it isn't the little scavenger bird!" said Mrs. Clifford as they stood in the study doorway. "Come in here, Cassandra. You will not cower behind Miss Jasper this time." Slowly Cass moved into the room, and Emily reached for Josie's hand. Whatever punishment Cass was given would be almost as unpleasant to witness.

Mrs. Clifford towered over her daughter. "How dare you," she hissed. "How *dare* you spoil this meal! Mr. Berringsley is not only my best patron, but he is a good man and entirely self-made. He came from nothing. He spent the Thanksgiving holidays of his childhood in an orphanage." Cass stood still as stone, staring up at their mother as she raged. "Can you imagine what it feels like to go to bed hungry? Of course not. You will never go to bed hungry while there are men like Mr. Berringsley to provide for you, Cassandra. And yet you could not wait one more hour until dinner. You broke into the pantry, like vermin, and ate your fill."

Emily squeezed Josie's hand, and she looked up and saw the tears in her tutor's eyes. Cass got into mischief like this all the time, but Mrs. Clifford was seldom so hard on her.

"Our friend Mr. Berringsley has a favorite dessert. Can you guess what it is, Cassandra? It is his favorite because it is the last sweet his poor mother ever made him."

Cassie glared at their mother. Her eyes were two

hot little coals burning in her head. "I wish *I* was an orphan."

Mrs. Clifford returned the glare. "What did you say?"

"I said I wish I was an orphan."

So swiftly there wasn't even time to flinch, Mrs. Clifford reached out and slapped her daughter hard enough to send Cass stumbling sideways into the desk. Emily bit back a cry of anguish. Josie drew a clean handkerchief out of her pinafore pocket and passed it to her.

"You're a greedy, ungrateful little chit," spat Mrs. Clifford. "I'm ashamed to call you my child." Now Cass was heaped like a rag doll on the Turkish carpet, her small hand pressed to her cheek. She wouldn't cry until she was back in the nursery, in Emily's arms. "I have told Mrs. Dowd to save the remnants of the pudding. You will eat every last morsel, without pause, if it takes you a week." She aimed a finger at the door. "Now go to the kitchen."

Cass got to her feet and walked out of the study, her eyes on the carpet all the way. Emily released Josie's hand and fled up the stairs. Josie remained in the doorway, watching as her mother calmly seated herself at the desk. Mrs. Clifford looked out the window and smoothed back a wisp of hair that had escaped its careful arrangement. Then she seemed to notice the presence of her elder daughter. "Why are you standing there like an imbecile? Go and find something useful to do before our guests arrive."

Josie tried to think of some retort, but her mother turned back to the window and the moment passed. So she went down the hall and into the kitchen, where Cass sat with the dessert bowl under the watchful eye of Mrs. Dowd. The bowl was massive, with enough pudding to feed eight people four times over. This time Cass had a spoon.

Josie watched her sister eat, thinking she might take over when the cook's back was turned to spare her the tummyache. But Mrs. Dowd said, "I'll not have you interferin' with that child's fair punishment. Now get yourself upstairs, Miss Josephine, and put on your good frock."

Her sister was too doggedly applying herself to the pudding—the taste of which had, no doubt, ceased to please that sharp little tongue—to receive Josie's parting glance of sympathy. She went upstairs and found Emily sitting on Cassie's bed, pressing her wet handkerchief to her eyes though her tears were more or less spent.

"She'll be sick," Emily whispered as Josie sat down beside her.

"She'll be all right," Josie said with a certainty she did not feel.

Cassie was still chained to the kitchen table when the guests arrived, and Mrs. Clifford would not allow her to join them in the dining room.

Mr. Berringsley was as cheerful and as awkward as usual. His sister, Miss Amelia Berringsley, had always been kind, but it was difficult to look at her when you spoke to her, for her eyes never pointed in the same direction. The tall, humorless men who accompanied them—Mr. Bridges and Mr. Gates, both of Manhattan—seemed to be business associates rather than friends. Emily and Josie seated themselves together, Emily flicking nervous glances through the kitchen doorway.

"And where is your laughing cherub?" Mr. Berringsley asked as they seated themselves around the bounty of roast turkey and raisin-studded sage filling, candied sweet potatoes and corned beef hash. "Mrs. Clifford's younger daughter is a delight," Berringsley said to his associates, who nodded politely. "I have never met a brighter, more clever, more amiable little girl. I have often told Mrs. Clifford she is destined for the stage." He turned back to Lavinia, too eager to notice the stiff unsmiling look on her face. "As a matter of fact, one of Amelia's friends at the conservatory was telling us just the other day that it is never too early to begin her elocution lessons."

"I'm afraid elocution lessons are out of the question for the time being. Cassandra has not behaved herself today," Mrs. Clifford replied. "Josephine, will you please give the blessing?" The saying of grace was something they only did in the Berringsleys' company. Josie got through the words as quickly as she could, hoping to avoid any mistakes in front of their guests. No one seemed to notice how perfunctory the blessing had been apart from Mrs. Clifford, who frowned at her. *None of us can do anything right,* Josie thought, *so is there any use trying?*

She ate mechanically, without pleasure. It felt wrong to feast beside Cassie's empty place.

Miss Berringsley turned to her hostess. "And how are your memoirs coming along, Lavinia? William tells me he has already contacted several publishers in New York on your behalf."

Josie stared at her mother. On her free afternoons Mrs. Clifford often locked herself in her study, and they could hear the clackety-clack of her Royal typewriter going for hours without pause. Why had she never told them she was writing a book?

"Ah, but her book is to be so much *more* than a

memoir, Amelia," Berringsley cut in. "As I have told you, it is to be a framework for the spiritual development of the human race."

Mr. Bridges and Mr. Gates were too busy savoring their dark meat to make any comment on this extraordinary statement. Mrs. Clifford cast a thin smile at Amelia Berringsley. "As always, William has been very generous. I am making good progress, thank you, Amelia."

Mr. Berringsley was midway through a not-very-interesting story about his recent travels in London when they heard a commotion in the kitchen. "Off with you!" cried Mrs. Dowd as the back door slammed. "Not on *my* floor!"

Emily let out a gasp of horror. "Please excuse me," she cried as she threw down her napkin and fled from the room.

Miss Berringsley seemed genuinely worried. "Why, whatever is the trouble?"

"I do hope you will forgive these domestic disturbances, gentlemen." No one could have mistaken Mrs. Clifford's laugh for natural mirth. "I am striving to teach my children the value of honesty, and of discipline, and at times such as these I fear my progress is slow indeed."

"May I be excused, Mother?" asked Josie.

"You may not," Mrs. Clifford retorted, and began a conversation with Mr. Bridges and Mr. Gates about the stock market that Josie couldn't have followed even if she'd wanted to.

At length Emily returned. Mrs. Clifford cleared her throat. "Yes, Miss Jasper?"

"She's not well, ma'am. I have put her to bed." Emily reapplied herself to her plate with the mournful resolve of a prisoner at his final meal, paying no attention to the conversation between Mrs. Clifford, the Berringsleys, and their guests. The girls excused themselves at the earliest opportunity, and went up to check on Cassie. The child was sleeping fitfully.

"She vomited on the lawn." Emily stroked the damp hair away from the little girl's face. "Poor dear. I *knew* this would happen." She sighed. "You know, Josie, that I have never been at ease in your mother's presence, but today was the first day I found myself afraid of her."

The day of truth came three days after Thanksgiving. Josie quivered with anticipation as her mother leafed through the first section at the breakfast table. They were only permitted to read the paper once Mrs. Clifford had finished, and it felt as if she'd never taken as long as she did today. Josie had told Emily of the newspaper pact, and her tutor was almost as eager as she was.

Finally, *finally*, her mother laid down the paper and went to her study. Cass climbed into Emily's lap as Josie snatched the news section and hungrily scanned the headlines. "It's true, all of it, every word . . . 125,000 soldiers mobilized across Europe . . . the Serbs retaking Krushevo . . . Kitchener and Italy . . ." Then she spotted Colonel Maitland, and, with an exultant laugh, read the dispatch aloud:

LONDON, Nov. 27.—Colonel Maitland of the Royal Naval Air Service jumped with a parachute today from an aeroplane which was 10,000 feet in the air. He landed safely.

Colonel Maitland has been experimenting with

projected developments of the aerial service, and arrived at the point where it was necessary to determine whether an airman could land safely by parachute from such a height.

"Some one has to do it," he said. "There is only one person I care to ask. I will make the attempt myself."

It took the Colonel fifteen minutes to make the descent, but he solved his problem satisfactorily.

Emily smiled. "That is what is called a dry sense of humor. Very British," she said to Cass, stroking the little girl's hair and resting the back of her hand on her forehead. "Still warm. You poor dear."

It was Sunday, but they returned to the nursery out of habit, and Josie hid the newspaper in the bottom drawer of her desk. Then she drew out a fresh sheet of stationery.

He Fell 10,000 Feet and
Landed Safely
16.

THIS IS FAR AND AWAY THE MOST EXCITING THING
THAT HAS EVER HAPPENED TO ME ALEC—

"Me too," he replied, grinning at the empty room. "I just wish I could write you back."

I HAVE ALREADY BEGUN A SECOND LETTER—BUT
WHERE SHALL I HIDE IT?

"Maybe you could keep them all in one safe place. I can look for them and once I find them I'll tell you where."

WHAT A SPLENDID IDEA ALEC—ONLY DONT READ
THEM ALL AT ONCE—

"And maybe you could save something else for me, too. Like a time capsule!"

Time capsules weren't a thing yet, but Josie promised to leave him a "treasure box," and on a weekend morning he went hunting for her letters, thinking over the conversations they'd had so far. The board didn't seem to work like a telephone, since she'd always been there to answer apart from that one time in his room. If their dates always matched, a hundred years to the hour, there would have been times when one found the other absent.

There were no hidden compartments in his closet. No loose floorboards either. Next, he took the cushion off the window seat, lifted the lid, and pulled out a stack of spare blankets. Now *here* would be the perfect place to hide something, provided no one else had found it in the intervening years. The compartment was lined in cedar wood, and he ran his fingers along the seams of the smooth red planks. There was a small notch at the edge of one of the planks, where the base of the cupboard met the side. Alec stuck his finger in and pulled, muttering "*yessssss!*" when the board yielded to his tugging.

There was a four-inch gap between the bottom of the storage compartment and the floor. He pulled out the wooden panel and laid it on the rug. It didn't look like there was anything but dead insects and dust bunnies in the hidden space, but he wouldn't expect her to leave anything so easy to find. He leaned into the chest, dipping his hand into the dark perimeter of the space, his fingertips trailing over splinters and globs of gray dust.

Finally he felt something soft but firm wedged between the cupboard base and the plank that kept it mounted above the floor, and he pried it free and brought it up into the light. The package was wrapped in oilcloth, and his heart thudded joyfully as he pulled off the covering and read his name on the first envelope in the stack. There were a dozen in all!

It was a mild sunny day, so rare for November, and he brought the first letter down to the back terrace tucked inside his school copy of *The Adventures of Huckleberry Finn*. This letter was longer than the one he'd found in the library, and when he finished it he felt he knew her better than ever. She gave him a scene-by-scene account of the Thanksgiving Day incident, and told how three days later Cass was still quiet and pale and couldn't eat much; of jolly Dr. Jennings, his English accent and his bizarre conversations with her mother's "spirit controls"; and of the suffrage rally, and "The Enchanted Head," and Mrs. Gubbins's prophecy that she would never marry. *Of course it is balderdash, but why did it affect me so? I don't know if you can understand why it upset me, being a boy,* she wrote. He kept all her letters in a shoebox, along with the notebook he used when they communicated—a little archive of his own.

"I don't think about growing up or getting married," he said a few nights later, once he'd told her of the hiding place beneath the window seat. "It's a long time from now, you know? Plus people get married a lot later now than they used to."

I THINK OF IT ALL THE TIME—IT IS DIFFERENT FOR US—IT IS AN ESCAPE—INTO AN EVEN MORE DIFFICULT CIRCUMSTANCE PERHAPS—BUT I SUPPOSE MOST WOMEN FIND IT A RISK WORTH TAKING—

"I wonder why your mother got married," he mused. "It seems like she didn't really have to, with a rich patron like Mr. Vandegrift, and then Mr. Berringsley."

I CANT IMAGINE HER FALLING IN LOVE WITH ANYBODY THE WAY HEROINES DO IN NOVELS—I WISH

I COULD REMEMBER MY FATHER—PERHAPS SHE WAS
DIFFERENT WHEN HE WAS ALIVE—

"Hey, you mentioned Dr. Jennings in your letter. I read about him in the archive, too. I was thinking about looking him up on the computer, to see if the spirit was right."

I AM TERRIBLY CURIOUS BUT EMILY SAYS NONE OF
US SHOULD KNOW TOO MUCH ABOUT THE FUTURE—

"Hold on a second." He grabbed his mother's iPad from the kitchen counter and did a Google search for "Henry Jennings." The first hit was the doctor's Wikipedia entry. *President of the New York branch of the American Society for Psychical Research, 1912-1919. Died 1919, aged 39.* "I found him. Do you want to know?"

NO—I MEAN YES—BUT DONT TELL ME THE DATE—

"I don't know how you're gonna take this," he said, "but Baldassare was right."

December came, and with it new traditions. Together Alec and his mother collected pine cones and spiky sweetgum seed balls from the bottom of the backyard, spray-painting them gold and silver for Christmas tree decorations. They arranged his grandfather's antique train set and all the little shops and houses in a circle around the base of the tree, and his mother remarked with satisfaction that sometimes nostalgia really is as nice as it used to be. Grammy Sal drove over from Bridgeport to stay for a weekend, and Alec helped her bake and decorate an army of gingerbread men. They showed up in his lunchbox, so cheerful and perfectly iced that it felt wrong to eat them.

Some nights he'd read another of Josie's letters with a flashlight under the blanket. Her whole life was spent inside the four walls of this house, but she never ran out of things to write about: what she'd learned of the places she wanted to visit someday, Stonehenge and Delphi, the Colosseum and the Pyramids; ridiculous things Cass (or Mrs. Gubbins) had said or done; and her memories of the year they'd lived in New York City. Alec shivered to read of a carriage-ride through a slum on the way to Mr. Berringsley's Wall Street office when an old woman with horrible red sores around her eyes reached into the cab, grabbed Josie's hand, and offered to tell her fortune.

She transcribed everything she could remember of the sessions with Dr. Jennings, and wrote that she didn't know if she believed in a "higher power," or an endless cycle of death and rebirth, or a lost continent at the bottom of the sea. *I think of all the civilizations that have come and gone: they had their gods, just as we have ours. Emily says it is only sensible to question and to doubt.*

His mother said nothing more about the talking board or the impossible letters. He knew she was uneasy, but she had so many other things to worry about right now that he thought she must have filed the whole business under "my son's overactive imagination." Sometimes when he thought of Josie he had to wonder if he was making her up, if he'd been so struck by her picture that he'd convinced himself of something that was utterly nuts.

But Danny believed in all of it, too, he *knew* the letters were as old as they appeared to be, and Alec took comfort in what Josie said about the sense in doubting. If you questioned your own convictions, you'd end up either smashing them or strengthening them, wouldn't you? Alec questioned his every day, but the Clifford girls were still there—still *here*, in a manner of speaking.

Talking to them made him happier than he'd been in what felt like forever, and that had to count for something.

The Pillywinkis
17.

Emily always chose the most entertaining bedtime stories, and one of their favorites was *She* by Sir Henry Rider Haggard. The tale of a priestess in a remote African cave who has waited two lonely millennia for the return of her reincarnated soul mate, Emily knew it was rather grown up for them, but she also knew that the descriptions of "She-who-must-be-obeyed"—the loveliest woman who ever lived—would thrill the girls to their very toenails. Night after night they clung to her as she read, rapt and rapturous, and went on begging for one more chapter until the hall clock tolled midnight. That book had been the highlight of their summer.

Now Emily returned from a weekend in Manhattan

with a gift from her uncle: *Ayesha*, the sequel to *She*. With great anticipation the girls set aside their Colored Fairy Books, but it soon became clear, even to Cass, that the sequel lacked the breathless sparkle of the original. Still they paid close attention, as to a dear old chum with whom they no longer had much in common.

The next morning, as the girls were dressing for breakfast, Mrs. Clifford stormed into the nursery. She held in her hands a hair comb, fashioned out of silver and inlaid with delicate blue and green stones. More than once Lavinia Clifford had declared the pair of combs, another of Mr. Berringsley's exotic gifts, her most precious possession. Now one of them was broken in two. "Who did this?" she shouted.

Josie looked to Cass, who had turned the color of a tombstone. Emily appeared in her bedroom doorway, eyebrows raised in alarm.

Mrs. Clifford flicked a glance between her daughters and cried out in frustration. "Of *course* it was Cassandra. Who else? You're always putting your sticky little fingers on things that don't belong to you." She brandished the two pieces of the broken comb. "This was an antique. More than a hundred years old. And you broke it and stuffed the pieces in a drawer. Did you think I wouldn't find them?"

"I only wanted to see what it would look like in my hair," Cass whispered. "I'm sorry."

"Oh, you *will* be, by the time I'm through with you!" Mrs. Clifford turned to Emily. "Miss Jasper, is it too much to ask that you keep your charge occupied with her schoolwork and prevent her causing such mischief?"

Emily respectfully averted her eyes. "No, ma'am."

"See that it does not happen again." Mrs. Clifford cast a finger at her younger daughter. "Cassandra, come with me." Cass backed away and huddled in the window seat with her rag doll, as if by removing herself to the furthest corner of the room she could somehow avoid the inevitable. Their mother pointed to the carpet beside her. "Cassandra. *Come here.*"

Cassie crumpled into herself and shook her head. Mrs. Clifford strode across the nursery and grasped her by the ear. "No!" Cassie cried, clinging to Mrs. Gubbins as her mother pulled her from the room. "Oh, please, let go! It hurts!"

Mrs. Clifford dragged her halfway down the front stairs to the landing, where a linen cabinet was built into the wall. The doors were fastened at the top with a simple wooden latch. "This is the place for you, since you have such an interest in other people's closets!" And she pushed her daughter in among the tidy stacks of linen, fastening the cupboard door behind her.

Emily followed them down the stairs, her pale hands fluttering like doves in a cage. "Oh, but Mrs. Clifford, isn't there—"

"You'll have no meals today, Cassandra," Lavinia was saying to the cabinet door. "Not until supper, and if any of you disobey me then she will go without supper as well. No one is to allow her out. Is that understood?"

"But Mother, what if she has to—"

"If I cared to hear your opinion, Josephine, I would ask for it."

"But Mrs. Clifford, how will I—" Lavinia stormed down the stairs, deaf to Emily's pleading, and slammed the study door behind her. Emily dropped onto the landing-step and hid her face in her hands. "This is even more dreadful than Thanksgiving dinner."

At least she has Mrs. Gubbins to keep her company, Josie thought.

This particular punishment had befallen poor Cass twice before, both times before Emily had come to live with them. On both occasions Cassie had cried herself to sleep in the darkness of the closet, passing in and out of consciousness throughout the day. When her penance had finally come to an end, Mrs. Pike announced in disgust that the little girl had wet herself.

On those two terrible days Josie would talk to her sister through the door, or sneak her a biscuit or a drink of water, but it had never occurred to her that she might settle herself on the stairs and read to her, as Emily proposed. Their tutor gathered herself together, went up to her bedroom, and returned with *Ayesha*. "If you're to be locked in there all day, then I must give you something to take your mind off your troubles. Cass?"

Cass sniffled. "Yes, Em?"

"Can you guess what I have in my hands?"

A pause. "Is it *Ayesha*?"

"Yes, little one." Josie brought down two foot-stools from the nursery for them to sit on, and Emily began to read. Leo, the hero, and Horace, Leo's dearest friend and guardian, had resumed their epic quest to find the faraway place where Leo's great love, Ayesha, had been reborn. After many months of travel through the Himalayas, they arrived at the gates of an ancient monastery, where they conversed on spiritual matters with a wise old abbot. But they must continue their quest, and it led them through the snowy mountains. "'Chapter four,'" Emily read. "'The Avalanche.'"

"What's an avanatch?"

Their tutor turned to address the linen closet door. "It's called an avalanche, dear. It's when there's too much snow on a mountain, and it all comes falling down in a big terrible heap."

Merritt appeared at the foot of the stairs. "The child is being punished," he said in his somber monotone. "What is the meaning of this?"

Emily drew herself up, clasped the book to her chest, and lifted her chin. "Mrs. Clifford employs me to educate her children," she said stiffly. "And that education must continue, even if one of my pupils is passing the day shut inside the linen closet."

For a moment Merritt regarded her as impassively as ever. Then he turned and went to the study door, and Mrs. Clifford's voice called, "Come in."

Josie sensed her tutor bracing herself for Mrs. Clifford's appearance, but she did not come, and in a few moments Emily had regained her rhythm. "'Oh, what a sight was that! On from the crest of the precipitous slopes above, two miles and more away, it came, a living thing, rolling, sliding, gliding; piling itself in long, leaping waves, hollowing itself into cavernous valleys, like a tempest-driven sea, whilst above its surface hung a powdery cloud of frozen spray . . .'"

"I can see it, Emily!" Cassie exclaimed. "When I close my eyes I can see the avanatch!"

The day wore on. Josie knit while Emily read, and Josie read while Emily darned a stocking. Cass kept up her barrage of questions, and Emily answered every one. When the rich scent of beef stew wafted upstairs and Mrs. Pike rang the bell for luncheon, the two girls glanced at each other and were resolved. Josie continued to read. Mrs. Clifford appeared at the foot of the stairs, watching and listening, but she did not interrupt them. When one of their stomachs growled they smiled grimly to each other and continued on.

Leo and Horace fell from a cliff and landed in an icy river where they were rescued from drowning by a beautiful and mysterious woman who carried herself like royalty. The queen—for queen she was—made love to Leo at every opportunity. "Don't listen to her, Leo," Cassie piped up. "She's a witch."

Emily let the book fall closed with her finger marking the place. "Why would you use that word, dear?"

"Mrs. Gubbins says 'sorceress' is just a fancy word for 'witch.'"

"Well, that's true."

"But she says you shouldn't use words like that when you don't really mean them. Sometimes there are bad men and if you don't do as you're told, they'll stick your fingers in the pillywinkis."

"What in heaven's name is a pillywinkis?" asked Josie.

She had no doubt her sister was shrugging in the darkness. "She hasn't told me yet."

"Why don't you ask her?" said Emily, disregarding Josie's incredulous look.

The little girl paused. "She says this is a relatively civilized age we are living in, and so she trusts we shall never know."

That night Josie felt the pull of the talking board, but she did not yield to it. Cass had been allowed out for supper, but their mother's mood had scarcely improved, and a midnight chat with her friend from the future would have been even more imprudent than usual. The following night she went down, and the planchette took off as soon as she touched it.

I HAVE MY FIRST APPOINTMENT WITH THE DOCTOR TOMORROW AND IM KIND OF NERVOUS—

"Why?" Josie leaned forward, as if she could

communicate her concern without words. "Are you ill?"

NOT THAT KIND OF DOCTOR—IM GOING TO A
PSYCHIATRIST—YOU KNOW WHAT THAT IS?

"A doctor for the mind," she said.

YUP EXACTLY—I HAVENT TOLD YOU THIS BEFORE
BUT MY PARENTS ARE GETTING DIVORCED—

I haven't seen my dad in two months. She'd been meaning to ask if he was employed away from home. "Oh," Josie said softly. "I'm so very sorry to hear that, Alec."

THANKS JOSIE—I GUESS WHEN PEOPLE GET
DIVORCED IN 1915 ITS STILL PRETTY SCANDALOUS BUT
HERE IT HAPPENS A LOT—WE WILL BE ALL RIGHT—
BUT LETS TALK ABOUT YOU NOW—

So Josie told him all about Cass spending the day shut inside the linen closet.

WHAT?—JOSIE ARE YOU SERIOUS?—

"It's true, I'm afraid. Mother has done it before, but that was before Emily came."

YOU KNOW THATS ABUSE RIGHT?—SO WAS MAKING
HER EAT PUDDING TIL SHE THREW UP—

"It *is* cruel," she said slowly. "I wish Mother would not let her temper get the best of her."

IF SOMEBODYS MOM DID THAT TODAY SHED BE
ARRESTED—

Josie didn't know what to say. It *was* horrid, but wasn't it also a mother's right to punish her child however she saw fit?

CAN EMILY DO ANYTHING TO HELP YOU?—

"Not if she wants to keep her position. And if Emily were to leave us, I don't know *what* I'd do. No," she sighed. "I can only coax Cassie into behaving like the good and obedient child I usually know her to be. To encourage her by example, I suppose." Josie's tongue tasted sour in her mouth. Was she as much of a priss as she sounded?

NOBODY CAN BE GOOD ALL THE TIME JOSIE—the pointer spelled out. ITS UP TO OUR PARENTS TO BE FAIR TO US EVEN WHEN WE ARENT GOOD—

Alec's mother had never locked him in a closet all day. She'd never let him go hungry, or call him an imbecile, or turn him away when all he wanted was her arms snug around him. Josie knew all this for certain.

Future Perfect
18.

There was something ever so slightly familiar about Dr. D'Amato—or Alonzo, since he insisted upon first names—as if Alec had met him once before, in one of those dreams that actually have a plot. Alonzo was as tall as a pro basketball player, he laughed more often than Alec would have expected from a psychiatrist, and his beard was so black it almost looked as if the man had drawn it on with a Sharpie. There was a little ceramic bowl with burning incense in the waiting room, and an enormous canvas above the sofa that looked as if the artist had played a few rounds of paintball.

Mrs. Frost came in and sat with them for the first few minutes, and Alec knew she was trying to get him to feel as comfortable as possible before she left to run her errands. When she went out, Alonzo turned to a fresh page on his yellow notepad and said, "Your mom is pretty cool, huh? I bet you're happy to be stuck with her."

Alec grinned in spite of his nerves.

"All right," Alonzo said. "Time to get real. Do you think there's something you could have done to prevent your parents' breakup?"

"Is that a trick question?"

"Nope."

"I mean, I *know* the answer's supposed to be 'no.'"

"Is it?"

"Are you one of those shrinks who turns everything back into a question?"

"I don't know. Do *all* your shrinks ask too many questions?"

Alec laughed.

"Don't read too much into it. Is there anything you feel like you could have done or done differently?"

Alec hesitated. "No."

"I'm asking because a lot of the time kids feel like there must be some way they've been inadequate. Unconsciously, of course. Like if they were more lovable their parents would be trying harder to stay together, even though that's totally not rational, right?"

"I guess."

"What's happening to your family now, these tectonic shifts, all this goes well beyond the realm of 'rational.' Your head can be telling you one thing while your heart's feeling something else." The doctor opened his top desk drawer. "Would you like to play a game?"

Alec gave the doctor a skeptical look, and Alonzo laughed. "I'm not conning you, I promise," he said as he drew out a pack of playing cards. "This really will be fun. Fun for me too, actually." Alonzo slid the cards out of the box, shuffled them a few times, fanned them out and offered them to Alec. "Pick one and leave it face down. Don't look at it yet." Alec chose a card. "Okay, now turn it over. Take a few moments to look at it, and then I want you to tell me the first thoughts that pop into your head."

Alec flipped the card and frowned. This wasn't a deck of ordinary playing cards at all. Instead of diamonds or spades the card had a color illustration of a small boy leaning out an open window, reaching for something beyond the confines of the picture. "Sometimes I feel like I don't belong here," Alec said.

"Where would you rather be?" Alonzo asked. "Where would you belong?"

Nineteen fifteen, he wanted to say—but if his mother hadn't told Alonzo about the talking board and Josie's letter, he wasn't about to bring it up. They already had plenty to talk about without Alonzo having to wonder if Alec was out-of-his-mind crazy. "Not *somewhere* else," he amended. "Some other time."

"Do you ever imagine what your life will be like in the future?" Alonzo asked.

"How do you mean? Like in high school, or when I'm grown up?"

The doctor smiled. "Either one. Both. It's fun to think about, isn't it?"

"I guess."

The therapist waited for him to elaborate. "*Do* you think about it, Alec?"

He opened his mouth to explain that the present was awful enough without taking all the terror of the future into account, too—that the past was the only place where things still made any sense—but he didn't know how to put words around it.

"Let me reframe the question," Alonzo said. "Imagine a year has passed. You're in seventh grade. Your dad has been doing his own thing for a good while now. You and your mom are used to your new life." He paused. "Do you think it will be easier to be happy—to have optimistic thoughts about the future?" Alonzo wagged his finger. "And don't just say 'I guess.' I really want you to imagine what life will be like."

Alec stared through the carpet, trying to picture himself two inches taller and generally quicker to smile. He knew he would grow older, taller, wiser, in theory, at least; yet the future still felt highly improbable somehow, like a country too dangerous to visit.

Two nights later Alec told Josie all about the session with Alonzo. "It was actually kind of fun," he said. "We played a card game, and he got me to talk about my feelings and stuff."

ARE YOU EVER LONELY ALEC?

"I guess I am, sometimes. But I don't really know what else to compare it to."

DO YOU EVER WISH YOU HAD A BROTHER OR SISTER?

"When I talk to you, I do," he replied, but his own words sounded out of tune somehow. He liked Josie better than he could imagine feeling about a sister, even a fun sister like Cass.

They spoke for hours, if you could call it speaking. It was only fair that she should ask most of the questions. *Tell me about your mother, your grandmother, your father, the house as it is then. Tell me how you've decorated it for Christmas. What color is the house now? Yellow? In our time it is dove-gray, with dark blue trim.* He told her about Grammy Sal's gingerbread men and the sweater she was knitting for him, and all about *Harry Potter*, because of course Josie didn't know what a Weasley sweater was.

OH—HOW I WOULD LOVE TO READ ALL THE GOOD
BOOKS YET TO BE WRITTEN—

When he wrote this down in his notebook he added
an exclamation point. That was how she must have said
it.

A Fancy Word for "Witch"
19.

Josie waited until the house was still—past eleven, by the chiming of the hall clock—and crept down the kitchen stairs to the reading room with her notebook and candle, a blanket slung over her arm as usual. She laid down the blanket to block the light and went to the cabinet. So intent was she on speaking to Alec that she'd brought the board to the table, settled herself in her chair and opened the notebook to a fresh page before she noticed she wasn't alone in the room.

Her mother sat in an armchair by the window. She might have been waiting there for hours. "What are you doing?" she asked in an even tone.

Josie's heart raced and her mouth went sour with the knowledge that nothing would be the same now. Everything was spoiled. Why, why, *why* hadn't she stayed in bed?

Mrs. Clifford rose and came into the light, wearing that look Josie now thought of as the sorceress's smile. *Mrs. Gubbins says 'sorceress' is just a fancy word for 'witch.'* Had there ever been a time when her mother hadn't gotten exactly what she wanted?

"Answer me, Josephine." There was no sternness in her voice, only satisfaction.

"I should think, Mother, that the answer to your question is self-evident."

Mrs. Clifford seated herself at the table opposite her daughter. "Then by all means, continue." She laid the glass pointer on the question mark, rested her graceful tapered fingertips upon it, and nodded to the open notepad on the far end of the table. Josie picked up the pencil without looking her mother in the eye. If she did, she might be too tempted to spit in it.

"Now then," said Lavinia Clifford. "Let us converse with your friend Alec."

"But how . . ." Josie sputtered. "How do you know his name?"

Again, she smiled that horrible smile in lieu of an answer.

It was excruciating, the hour that followed. The pointer sprung into motion, directed to HELLO before spelling her name, as it always did. Josie opened her mouth, but her mother shushed her.

"Good evening, Alec. I understand you are alive and well in the twenty-first century. I have been anticipating this conversation for quite some time." Again the pointer began to move.

THIS ISNT JOSIE—

"Alec, I'm here. But my—"

Her mother reached across the board and slapped

her hand. "I believe that we have been granted this chance to communicate for a higher purpose, Alec. I wish to share this miracle with the world. Will you help me in this noble work?"

PLEASE MAAM—ID LIKE TO TALK TO JOSIE—

"Josie has been using the talking board without my permission. I will not allow her to do so again."

PLEASE JUST LET ME TALK TO JOSIE—

"I will permit you to speak to her once you have answered certain questions to my satisfaction. Will you co-operate?" Slowly, reluctantly, the pointer moved to YES.

Alec answered all the questions she asked him. A temperance bill would pass in 1919, though people would go on drinking as much as before, and national women's suffrage would pass the following year. America would enter the war, and win, and President Wilson would be awarded the Nobel Peace Prize. Josie began to wonder if he were reading from his history book. It was so much to remember, and she knew she herself couldn't have described in such detail the political events of a hundred years before.

Soon her mother grew impatient with the near future, finding it too much as she had expected. She wanted to hear of the flight industry, and the trip to the moon, and all the presidents yet to be born. Have the people of the future found the way to world peace? No? Then how many more wars would there be in the next hundred years? Where, and why, and who would prove victorious?

Josie wrote everything down, alternately stunned by the future taking shape beneath her pencil and itching for the moment she'd be able to apologize for her mother's behavior. *Mother will ask him just one more question,* she kept thinking, *and then she'll allow me to talk to him.*

IVE ANSWERED YOUR QUESTIONS MRS CLIFFORD—
NOW WILL YOU PLEASE LET ME TALK TO JOSIE?

"Some other time, perhaps." Lavinia Clifford lifted the pointer and moved to pick up the board.

Josie brought her hand down on the wooden panel. "But you said I could talk to him once you'd—"

Mrs. Clifford slid the board out from under her palm and brought the pieces back to the cabinet. "I said *some other time,* Josephine. Now go up to bed."

Mrs. Clifford was still in bed the afternoon after her latest session with Dr. Jennings. On the morning of the doctor's departure they saw Mrs. Pike bring up the customary tray of tea and broth, and Josie resolved to take advantage of the situation.

"I want to talk to Dr. Jennings," she whispered across the dining table. Emily opened her mouth to reply, but Josie went on, "Not here. I want to talk to him where *she* can't hear us. At the hotel."

"Why do you want to talk to him?"

"I want to tell him about Alec." There was more to it than that. Perhaps the doctor could advise her on this new problem of her mother's interference.

Emily nodded, and when the housekeeper came in to clear the breakfast dishes she told Mrs. Pike that they were going for an early walk.

The girls put on their coats and went out into the blustery morning. The Manningford Inn had a porch that wrapped around all four sides, and it was by the front railing that Josie met Mabel Foley, in a circle of girls all in the green uniform of the Day School.

Josie's heart beat queerly, as if she had committed some wrongdoing and had just been found out. "Why, hello, Mabel."

Mabel cast a glance to her friends on either side before returning the greeting. "Good morning," she said, and immediately pressed her fingers to her lips. A moment later, when their party of three had passed through the front door, Josie understood why: peals of laughter rippled through the group, followed by a chorus of whispers.

As they entered the hotel lobby she took Emily's other hand, and squeezed it hard. "Don't give them another thought," her tutor murmured. "Sometimes your mother is right."

There was a crimson velvet borne sofa at the center of the hotel lobby, the novelty and elegance of which Cass could not resist. Emily and Josie left her sitting quietly, running her hands back and forth over the plush velvet seat, Mrs. Gubbins in her lap.

They found the doctor in the dining room, absorbed in the newspaper over the remnants of his sausage and eggs. "Aha! Miss Clifford!" he said, though he didn't seem at all surprised to see her.

Emily laid a hand on Josie's shoulder. "May we join you, Doctor?"

"It will only take a minute," Josie rushed to add. He gestured to the two empty chairs across the table, and the girls seated themselves.

As she took her chair, Emily made certain she could see Cassie through the doorway. "We heard you are leaving for the city this morning, Dr. Jennings."

"I am, indeed. Miss Whipple went by the early train." The doctor folded the newspaper and laid it on the table beside his plate.

"But you will be back?"

"Oh, certainly. Mrs. Clifford and her coterie of spirits have not finished with me yet." Dr. Jennings hailed a passing waiter. "Tea, for my guests," he said. "Now, to what do I owe this delightful surprise?" He smiled as he poured himself what was left of the coffee in his carafe.

Josie stared at him. Then she blurted, "I hide in the back hall so I can hear everything. I was there when she told you about Viola." She regretted saying as much as she watched the smile fall from his face, but there was no help for it now. "I can't manage it every time you come, but I have seen and heard things very few people would believe. Including myself," she added, "and I *did* see it."

Dr. Jennings looked to her tutor and raised an eyebrow. "And you permit this, Miss Jasper?"

Emily gave him a wry little smile. "My purpose is to encourage her curiosity, sir—in whatever form it takes."

The doctor echoed her smile and turned to Josie. "Was there something you wished to ask me? About something your mother said in trance, perhaps?"

"Not exactly. Dr. Jennings, I have been making my own . . . how shall I put it . . . experiments into the true nature of the spirit world, and you are the only person I can think of who might understand." The doctor nodded, and she continued. "I have been using my mother's talking board to converse with someone I believe to be living in our house a very long time from now."

The doctor frowned. "Someone living in your

house—in the future?" Josie nodded. "And what has this entity communicated to you, to allow you to think so? You are utterly convinced, I can see that."

"He knows things about our family, things even I didn't know. My mother isn't exactly forthcoming."

Again the doctor nodded, with a faint smile of amusement. "And how did he claim to know these details about your family?"

"He says he has been to the public library, that there is an archive there. A box of materials relating to my mother's mediumship. That's how he knew about *you*, Dr. Jennings. He read about you in one of the Spiritualist magazines." She remembered Baldassare's prophecy, and felt a pang of sadness as she met the doctor's eye. "I know that doesn't sound like proof of anything, but he told me those magazines are falling to pieces. They're a hundred years old."

Dr. Jennings stroked his beard as he listened. "I see. What other evidence did he offer?"

The waiter brought the tea and poured them each a cup as Josie told the doctor about the newspaper of November 28th. "He told me every single caption, two weeks in advance," she said. "Not a word out of place."

"Extraordinary," murmured the doctor.

"Oh, please don't say it like that, sir." Josie picked up her teacup, paused, and set it down again. "You must admit that even if he'd merely predicted them, as my mother is wont to make predictions in her trance state, they are never as detailed as a word-for-word headline." She took a sip of her tea. "Not even the most gifted prophet could be so precise."

"And you believe the most rational explanation is that they were not, in fact, predictions at all." She nodded, and the doctor leaned back in his chair, staring

131

at a point somewhere above her head. "I must say, Miss Clifford, this is downright fascinating, and I assure you I am not merely saying so to indulge you. Does the gentleman purport to be from the twenty-first century?"

She nodded. "From the year two thousand fifteen. And he's just my own age."

"And he claims he is living in your house?"

She nodded. "He says the great cabinet in the reading room is still there, and that he found the talking board in the drawer."

"I have never heard the like of this. It is a fantastic story, and if it is true then it changes absolutely everything we know of the nature of time. We must always employ scientific methods in our investigations, however, and guard against the pitfalls of wishful thinking."

"Oh, but I didn't *wish* he WAS from the future," Josie replied quickly, and Emily gently tapped her hand. She was speaking too loudly. "At first I thought he was a restless spirit," she whispered.

"I must admit it seems unlikely you will gather the empirical evidence needed to prove your hypothesis beyond all reasonable doubt," he went on. "I imagine, though, that if it is true, your friend from the future has ample evidence on *his* side of things." He chuckled.

"He has my letters," Josie said. "He tells me where he finds them, and that's how I know where to hide them."

"If all this is true, it would indicate that future events can influence what is past. But I am afraid we cannot discount the possibility of telepathy."

"I may never be able to prove it," said Josie. "But I believe it. I *know* it."

"Faith and science are as oil and water," said the

doctor, but he was smiling.

Emily cast a nervous glance over the doctor's shoulder. Cassie had tired of petting the velvet sofa, and was now wandering around the lobby murmuring to Mrs. Gubbins as she pointed at pictures on the wall. "I do apologize, Doctor." Emily took one last sip of her tea, rose from her chair and gathered her purse. "I think we had better be getting back to our schoolroom. Thank you very much for the tea, and for your kind and attentive ear." Josie's tutor laid a hand on her shoulder. "We'll wait for you in the lobby, dear."

The doctor drew a tin of Altoids out of his pocket and popped it open. "Peppermint?"

"No, thank you."

He laid a mint on his round, red tongue. "I will tell you a thing I read in one of those magazines once. It was an odd little piece concerning the cadavers of blind men. Do you know what a cadaver is, Miss Clifford?"

"A corpse, sir."

"Indeed. And do you know what an autopsy is?" Josie shook her head. "When a person dies, a doctor may study the remains if the cause of death is unknown or unclear. A still heart may yet have much to tell. The other organs too, of course. That is known as an autopsy. I go to the trouble of explaining this to you because the article concerned the posthumous study of blind men's fingers. Can you guess what they found inside the blind men's fingertips?"

"I'm sure I couldn't, sir."

Doctor Jennings leaned across the table. His breath smelled strongly of peppermint. "Gray matter," he murmured, his eyes alight. "Brain cells. They thought with their fingers!"

"Marvelous," she sighed.

He held up a warning finger. "Aha! No, Miss Clif-ford. It is *not* marvelous. It is *science*." The doctor drew out his billfold and laid a dime on the table. "There is no such thing as magic. It is simply science we have yet to comprehend."

It's just technology. "And is that not a matter of faith, Dr. Jennings?"

A smile was his only answer. They rose from the table and went into the lobby, where Cassie grew suddenly bashful and hid in Emily's skirts. Josie felt a twinge of desperation as the doctor opened his mouth to take his leave. "Dr. Jennings?"

The doctor seemed to understand, and stepped aside to hear her parting words. "Mother has discovered us," she said in a low voice, darting glances here and there. (How she hoped she would not see Mabel a second time!) "I am so afraid my friend and I will never speak in privacy again. She—she wishes to *use* him."

The doctor's eyes narrowed, and again she caught a whiff of mint when he said, "I must say, that does not surprise me." He regarded her with a frank look. "You are very like your mother, you know. And I do not mean that unkindly." Then something else seemed to occur to him. "Have you kept records of these conversations?"

"Yes, of course, sir."

"Very good. You have the makings of a psychical researcher! Now, if you'll excuse me—I'm very sorry, but I must not miss the ten o'clock train." He took a step forward again, and bowed. "Miss Clifford—Miss Jasper—Miss Cassandra," he said, smiling to each of them. "I shall see you all on my next visit to Edward-stown."

A Very Impertinent Young Man
20.

Lavinia Clifford had taken over the board, Alec understood that much, but had Josie been punished for it? Would they ever be allowed to speak again without her mother barging in and asking questions? The more he'd told her the more uneasy he'd felt. There wasn't any point knowing that much about the future—unless, of course, she meant to use it somehow, and he wanted no part of that. There were no answers to be found in Josie's letters. He'd already read the last of them.

The next morning his mother greeted him again with her *we-need-to-talk* face. "Your dad would like to see you this weekend."

"Well, *I* don't want to see *him*."

"Please, Alec. You're not going to see him for

Christmas this year. It's only fair."

Alec gave her a look: *don't talk to me about "fair."*

"I know," she sighed. "I know. But please try, okay? I told him we'd take the train into the city for the day, and I'll do some shopping while you're having lunch."

"Can Danny come too?"

"Aw, sweets. I'm sure that would be fun, but I think your dad would prefer to talk to you one on one."

That was the very *last* thing Alec preferred to do. "I don't want to go unless Danny comes too."

Mrs. Frost paused. "I'll talk to your father and see what he says."

His father had agreed—reluctantly—to Danny joining them for lunch, and they arrived at the Italian restaurant a few blocks off Times Square fifteen minutes early. "Be good," his mother said. "Grand Central at six sharp, all right?"

"You aren't going to wait with us?"

"I'm sorry, sweets," she whispered in his ear. "It'll be easier for us both if I don't."

When his father arrived, Alec saw why his mother hadn't wanted to stay. Mr. Frost gave him an awkward hug, offered Danny an even more awkward handshake, then took the hand of the young woman standing next to him. She wore very high heels, red lipstick, and a fur coat, and Alec hated her immediately. "Alec, I'd like you to meet Ariana," his father was saying.

"You didn't tell me you were bringing someone."

"Now don't be rude, son. Can you please say hello to Ariana?"

No, Alec thought as he watched the frown deepen on his father's face. *No, I will not say hello to Ariana.*

Alec's feet carried him out the door, and he did not stop running 'til he'd rounded the corner onto Eighth Avenue. He wasn't even aware of Danny running after him until the two of them fell against a plywood wall papered over with concert flyers, gasping for breath.

Danny began to laugh, softly at first, and then ever louder and more uproariously until people passing by began giving them concerned looks. "That was actually kind of awesome," he said, still clutching his stomach. "You should have seen the looks on their faces!"

"I don't care," Alec said. His father hadn't played fair, so why should he? There was another feeling, too, gently nosing its way up through the anger. He felt *good*. Captain of his own ship, as Josie might have put it. He threw up his hands, spun around and whooped. It was almost like he'd grown six inches since running out of that restaurant, like he knew beyond all doubt that he and Josie would be able to talk again.

Danny shot him an impish look. "So what do you wanna do now?"

Alec's phone buzzed. It was his mom, and he knew why she was calling. "I couldn't do it," he said. "We're going to have an adventure instead. See you at six, Mom. I love you!" He ended the call without letting her get a single word in. He knew he was in trouble, but there were almost six hours of perfect freedom between now and then.

They stopped for falafel on a street corner and ate it in Bryant Park, the walkways lined with temporary holiday shops selling soap made from volcanic ash and toys out of recycled milk bottles. The city presented itself to him very differently now that he no longer lived here: everything was as loud and as colorful as ever, everyone moving as quickly and impatiently as they always had, but it all passed *around* him rather than *through* him, like it used to. It helped that Danny had never lived in the city, and was delighted by everything and everyone they met. "If you were a time traveler spending a few days in 2015," he asked, "where would you hang out?"

Alec paused to reflect, as if this were a completely serious question. "I guess that would depend on whether the time traveler's from the future or the past."

Danny scoffed. "There aren't any time travelers from the past!"

"How do *you* know? Maybe somebody invented time travel a long time ago and kept it a secret."

"Yeah, like Leonardo da Vinci," Danny said. "That dude invented *everything*."

They decided that if Leonardo were vacationing at the tail end of 2015 he'd want to spend his first afternoon at the Wonder Lab—the Met, of course, was much too predictable—so they walked back uptown to 56th Street. *Please, please, please,* he found himself thinking as they watched a dozen life-sized robots sing "The Holly and the Ivy" with all the quirks and gestures of real people. *Please let me have the chance to tell her all about this.*

Christmas night Alec crept down to the reading room wearing his new headlamp and brought the talking board out of its hiding place. "Hello?" he whispered. The pointer sprung to life.

HELLO ALEC—

"Josie?"

IT IS I YOUR FRIEND OF THE NONE TOO RECENT

Alec hesitated. "Merry Christmas!" he said, with more enthusiasm than he felt. "Did you get any nice presents?"

WHAT IS THE PURPOSE OF ASKING FOR THINGS YOU DONT NEED FROM A MAN WHO DOESNT EXIST?——

Alec's heart lurched. He'd *known* it wasn't Josie, only he'd wanted too badly for it to be her. "*You're* the one who talks to ghosts for a living!"

AND YOU ARE A VERY IMPERTINENT BOY ALEC FROST——

His newfound courage abandoned him as quickly as it had arrived. *How did she know his name?*

THEY TOLD ME YOUR NAME CLEVER BOY——the pointer spelled out——AND I KNOW WHERE IN MY HOUSE YOU LAY YOUR HEAD——

His pulse pounding in his eardrums, Alec dropped the glass pointer onto the carpet and froze, half convinced it would leap back onto the table. "You don't scare me, Lavinia Clifford," he declared to the empty room, but the words made him sound much braver than he felt.

The End of the World
21.

Josie was pulling on her stockings when Mrs. Pike came in with a tray full of their usual breakfast: two cups and a steaming teapot, and two plates of poached eggs, bacon, and toast. She set the tray on their school table and turned to leave. "Mrs. Clifford says you're to have breakfast in the nursery."

Cassie sat up in bed. "But why? We never eat in our room."

"You'll do as you're told." Mrs. Pike slammed the bedroom door behind her.

Cassie hopped out of bed, sat at the table, and began to butter her toast. "What does it mean?"

"I don't know." The door to Emily's room was closed. Josie knocked softly. "Em? Are you there?" She turned the knob, and found it locked. At first she was merely confused by these irregular happenings. Now she was frightened.

It was too quiet downstairs. Usually at this time of the morning they could hear the housekeeper setting the table in the dining room, and Mrs. Clifford giving orders for luncheon and supper. Josie sat on the window seat, too anxious to look at her breakfast.

An old-fashioned hackney, the kind you could hire at the train station, pulled up to the curb behind an old black horse. Through the skeletal branches of the maple tree Josie watched the driver dismount and open the carriage door. Cassie came over and pressed her nose to the glass.

The front door opened and Merritt and Emily appeared, striding toward the carriage. Merritt carried her suitcase, his free hand locked on their tutor's elbow.

Josie threw open the sash and stuck her head out into the chilly morning air. "Emily! Where are you going?"

Emily turned and lifted her head, but Josie got only a glimpse of her face before Merritt jerked her by the arm. Two young footmen appeared below the window, carrying a large steamer trunk between them.

The initials on the lid were done in gold leaf, and they glinted in the light as the trunk was conveyed swiftly to the hackney:

E.A.J.

The realization turned her stomach. "No!" Josie shouted. "No!" She threw open the bedroom door and raced down the stairs with Cass at her heels. Their mother was standing with Mrs. Pike in the hall, but Josie ignored them. She reached the threshold, but two pairs of hands restrained her with no semblance of gentleness.

Merritt handed the suitcase to the hackney driver, and Emily climbed into the cab. Mrs. Pike snatched at Cass with one hand, but the little girl was too quick. She ran down the walk—clad only in her nightdress!—how Josie could have laughed at that—and dodged Merritt in her pursuit of the carriage. He grabbed her arm, but she lunged forward and held out her free hand. Emily removed her glove to reach out and clasp it, then looked to Josie at the front door. She had seen that expression on her tutor before: it was a brave face, yet it concealed very little. "Goodbye, little one. I shall miss you more than words can say."

Josie made another attempt to free herself, but her mother and Mrs. Pike renewed their grip. "Let go of me! Emily! No!"

The footmen fastened Emily's luggage to the rack. Josie saw Merritt slip the driver his payment, despite Cassie still struggling against him. The man nodded to Merritt, and as the hackney pulled away Emily put her head out the window and held up a hand in final farewell. Cass began to cry, but Merritt did not release her until the cab was out of sight.

In all her life Josie had never felt such anger. It welled up from her gut like molten lava, her skin burned, and she felt her heart pounding against her face. Mrs. Pike let go of her arm, and she turned on her mother and scratched at the hand that still gripped her at the wrist. "I hate you!" Mrs. Clifford only smiled in her serenely maleficent way, and it made Josie loathe her all the more.

Merritt dragged Cassie back to the house by her elbow. She stumbled on a branch lying in the sidewalk, fell to her knees and stayed there, sobbing and sniffling as the blood from a scuffed knee seeped through her nightgown. Merritt looked down at her as if she were a wild animal lying wounded in the road. Josie ran down the steps and helped her sister to her feet.

"Come, come," said their mother as they went grudgingly inside. "We have had quite enough melodrama for one day."

The one good thing about the worst day of your life is that, by definition, all the days to follow are bound to be better; but that is not much comfort while you are in the thick of it.

Josie cleaned the blood from her sister's knee and helped her change into a fresh nightgown. Soon after their retreat there had been a murmured conference at the nursery door, and their mother said to Mrs. Pike, "They'll come out when they're hungry enough."

"I want Emily," Cass sobbed, pounding her fist against the pillow. "*I—want—Emily!*"

They huddled together in Cassie's bed and cried, and then they slept, and when they awoke they found the early afternoon was just as gloomy as the morning. They picked at their breakfast, drinking the cold oversteeped tea, and Josie read aloud from *The Crimson Fairy Book*. They wouldn't leave the room that day. "We'll never see her again, will we?" Cass asked.

"Don't say that. Someday we'll be all grown up, and we can do whatever we like, and then we'll go to New York and find Emily and we'll be happy."

"Promise?"

"I promise," Josie said solemnly.

The girls lay there on the bed in silence for a minute or two, and Josie lifted her hand to smooth the hair out of her sister's face. Then Cassie perked up and locked eyes with her doll, who was seated at the foot of the bed. Josie knew that look. "Are you listening to Mrs.

Gubbins?"

Cassie nodded. "She says Mother is afraid."

"Afraid? Of what?"

Cassie turned to the doll. "Afraid of what, Mrs. Gubbins?" She waited for the answer. "Afraid of the bad men. Not just the men who cut her with the knife and threw a brick through the window. Other people. Afraid of bad men putting on innocent faces and coming back to hurt her."

"What do you mean, 'putting on innocent faces'?"

Cass paused. "She sees knives where there are only fingers, and fangs where there are only teeth, and shadows where there is nothing to cast them."

Josie stared at her, open mouthed. "Where . . . how . . . how ever did you think of such a thing, Cass?"

"I *told* you," said Cass. "Mrs. Gubbins. She says we should take heart and be careful, because fear is catching."

On the second day they came down to breakfast, betrayed by their growling stomachs. Once the meal was cleared Mrs. Clifford led Josie into the reading room and shut the doors. She took a seat at the table and eyed her daughter expectantly.

Josie folded her arms tightly across her chest. "Why did you do it?"

"Don't be thick, Josephine. You know perfectly well why I dismissed her."

"No, Mother, I don't."

"You've been keeping secrets. It's a nasty habit, and Miss Jasper encouraged it." Her mother laughed a hard little laugh. "The three of you and your petty conspiracies. You were always going about as if I didn't know."

"Was it because she took me to see Dr. Jennings?"

"That was the final straw, yes."

"I only wanted to ask him what he thought of the talking board."

"My dear, I don't care if you discussed the price of beans in Timbuktu. I did not pay Miss Jasper to indulge your every whim, nor to encourage you to tell me falsehoods. Her conduct was thoroughly unladylike, and no reasonable person could argue the point."

The door creaked open, and Cass peeked inside. "But what about our studies?" Josie asked as her sister stood beside her.

"I shall find you a new tutor, and in the meantime I expect you to direct yourself as well as Cassandra. She has yet to learn her basic arithmetic, and her penmanship is atrocious. For the first time in your lives, I shall expect you to show some measure of discipline." Mrs. Clifford pointed a finger. "And there will be no more secrets between us. Is that understood?"

The girls nodded.

"Now," said Mrs. Clifford, settling herself in her chair, "if you would be so good as to take out the talking board and bring it here."

Josie groaned aloud as her mother pointed to Cassie. "Go to your room."

Cass stamped her foot. "I want to talk to Alec, too!" she cried, but with a nod from their mother Merritt clutched her around the middle with his cold, massive hands, lifted her four feet into the air, and conveyed her, squirming and whining, out of the room. Mrs. Clifford locked both doors and seated herself again.

JOSIE? ARE YOU THERE?

"I'm sorry, Alec." She began to cry, hiding her eyes so she would not have to see the look on her mother's face. "I'm so sorry."

145

"Now, then, Alec Frost," Lavinia began. "If you would be so good as to resume just where we left off the last time we spoke."

They tiptoed into Emily's room hoping to find forgotten things to remember her by. The door to the little cupboard in the wall stood ajar, and inside they found a hat ribbon and one of the tortoiseshell combs she'd worn in her hair. On the nightstand was her crumbling copy of *A Vindication of the Rights of Woman*, pages foxed and lightly annotated in pencil.

"I hate this," Josie said. "I hate feeling as if she's died." She hadn't realized just how much she'd been hoping for a letter of farewell until they'd been through every nook and corner of the room. But then, Mrs. Clifford hadn't given her time to write one.

The girls went back into the nursery and sat down at the school table. "We won't ever get to talk to Alec alone again, will we?"

"I don't know, Cass."

"It's so mean of Mother to take away our two best friends. I told that to Mrs. Gubbins and she said life isn't meant to be easy or fair, because if it were always easy and fair then there wouldn't be any point to it. Are you still going to write to him?" Josie nodded. "Well, I'm going to write him too, and you can put them in with the other ones in your hiding spot." So they each took out a fresh sheet of stationery, and began to write.

Dear Alec,

I am miserable at the thought that she has parted us for-ever. Why do terrible things always happen in clumps? First Mother sent Emily away—how I am sick in my soul at the thought of never seeing her again!—and now she will not cease asking about all the things she has no earthly right to know.

But I must keep writing, even when I have no way of knowing if you will receive these letters. You do know, don't you, that I used the board that night only because she compelled me? I can see what she wants—to make a prophet of you, and let the world believe she has come by your prophecies through her own "channels." I despise her for it, but I see no alternative. She told me if I didn't oblige her, I'd never use the board again. Now that threat looks as if it will come to pass, the same outcome as if I'd denied her, and so every day I wish I had.

Cassie misses you, too. I have enclosed a letter from her.

Your friend,
Josie

She tried not to smirk as she read over Cassie's letter. How curious it was, feeling this impulse to laugh when the only good parts of life had soured in the span of a few days.

Now—where to hide these new letters? She'd already crammed the first set of envelopes into the narrow space beneath the base of the window seat, and those were the only letters Alec had discovered so far. And yet, if she were to leave this last letter alongside the others, perhaps there was a chance he would find it in time.

In time? In time for what? She'd give anything to

undo the night she'd walked straight into the trap her mother had laid for her, but some things truly *were* impossible.

Still she must try it. Josie lifted the window seat and emptied the chest of its blankets before removing the bottom. Then, bending over the lip of the cupboard with the letter half concealed in the space beside the others, she lost her footing and hit her head against the lid of the chest, and the involuntary motion of her own fingers sent the letter into the dusty darkness.

She drew herself up again, rubbing the tender spot on her forehead. So *that* was why he hadn't found it.

One Last Letter
22.

He tried the talking board again and again, and each time Josie's mother came through and either grilled him for information about the future or taunted him as she had on Christmas night. "I'm not telling you anything else," he said before giving up on the board for good. "You never kept your word."

He and Danny went over every inch of the two adjoining rooms, feeling along the baseboards and checking the same loose flooring. There had to be more letters. There *had* to be. Both of them were afraid, though neither said so, that what they were looking for was locked in the cupboard in the wall.

Headlamp cinched to his forehead, Alec pulled out the bottom of the window cupboard and climbed inside, covering his nose as the dust swirled up around him. Here—he ran his fingers along the narrow space—was the place she'd hidden the first set. Now he angled his head so the lamp shone beyond it, into the darkest space inside the wall—and he saw it, a new letter, pale and waiting under a layer of dust. He couldn't aim the light and reach at the same time, and he groped and grasped at the darkness. If he were taller, with longer arms, that letter would be in his hands by now. Danny ran down to grab a yardstick from the garage.

A few minutes later Alec sat on his shins inside the window seat, filthy and triumphant. He didn't even wait to climb out before reading the letter. It was dated March 31, 1916, and began with *I am miserable at the thought that she has parted us for-ever.* The second page was a letter from Cassie.

Deer Alec,

We ar so sad sins Mother took the spirit bord away. Missis Gubbins says in some familys the appels fall very far from the tree indeede and in this we are forchunit. I uppose Josie told you Emily wint away to. We are so loanly now! I wantd to ask you so many kwestyons about the futyur but I uppose now I shall never get anuther chans. I hope I live to be a very old wumman so you can come and visit me wen I am very old. I hope you will stil recogneyes me then.

Your fiend,
CASS CLIFFORD

There was a postscript from Josie: *I know I really ought to have her work on her spelling, but it's so amusing I just can't bring myself to correct her.* Danny read the letter and laughed out loud.

If only he'd found this envelope along with the others! But then, was there any use wishing? He sighed as he put everything back in the chest. If they could've changed it, there wouldn't have been any letter to find.

Children of the Infinite
23.

Dr. Jennings returned to Edwardstown, but the girls were ushered back to the nursery right after breakfast every morning for three days, and Mrs. Pike turned the key in the lock. Josie paced the floor, devoured alternately by curiosity and resentment. She knew full well she might never have the chance to speak with the doctor again, but if only she could meet his eye, to communicate without words the truth of their distress!

In the meantime, she slipped her feet into Emily's shoes, and found them too big to fill. Cass laughed at her when she brought out the elementary readers, or designed an exercise by which the little girl might practice her letters. For hours her sister hunched over their study table, drawing pictures of dragons and pirate ships and men with suits of quills like a porcupine, as Josie sat on the window-seat reading the books Emily had left on the nursery shelves: *Dr. Jekyll and Mr. Hyde, Little Women, Jane Eyre, Uncle Tom's Cabin*. Emily had loved these stories, and turning the pages gave Josie a certain amount of comfort. Now and again she looked up from her reading to watch a motorcar pass or a bird alight on a branch in the leafless maple tree. *Where are you, Emily? New York, I suppose, but what are you doing? Are you thinking of us?*

At night they climbed into Emily's old bed, and Josie would reread their favorite stories.

Cass nodded off with her arm wrapped tightly around Mrs. Gubbins, and, a short time later, when Josie gave herself up to sleep, she'd tuck the book of fairy tales in the folds of the pinwheel quilt as if it were a good-luck charm. Sometimes she woke in the blackest hour of the night and the old panic would revisit itself upon her, lonelier and more horrible than ever. Emily was gone, and it was all her fault.

Gathering small items for Alec's time capsule gave her something to pass the hours—after all, there was no hurry—and he might receive it even if she would never know. So Josie found an old candy tin, emptied it of bric-a-brac, and began to look for things Alec might like. Cass watched her from the school desk, a green crayon poised in her little fist. "Can I help you fill the treasure box?"

"Of course you can."

Her sister offered a blue kazoo and a spinning top she'd once found in a Cracker Jack box, along with a fistful of peppermints saved from Mr. Berringsley's last few visits. Everything went into the tin with the smiling pigtailed girl and her dachshund labeled BARNABY'S BEST LEMON CANDIES. "Where are you going to put it?" Cass asked.

Josie tapped her finger on her nose, thinking. "Do you have an idea?"

Cass pointed through the open doorway at the little cupboard that had been Emily's. "Mrs. Gubbins says Alec will receive everything we put in there."

The following afternoon they were expecting Dr. Jennings, but as Mr. Berringsley was also visiting that evening, Mrs. Pike was needed in the kitchen and did not follow the girls to their room. Leaving Cass to her drawings and her whispered one-way conversations with Mrs. Gubbins, Josie crept down the back stairs while the women were out mopping the back porch and crouched in the darkened corridor outside the reading room door.

The doorbell chimed and two women entered the room, neither of whom wore black, followed by the doctor and his secretary. The sitters were slim and dark haired, relatively young women. Whoever they had lost, it must have happened some time ago.

Mrs. Clifford kept them waiting ten minutes before she took her seat at the table. Soon her chin fell to her chest and her head rolled to one side. When the medium spoke, it was in a voice Josie hadn't heard for some time. "I greet thee, O Women of the New World!"

One of the ladies bent to the ear of Dr. Jennings. "Which one is this, Doctor?"

Josie heard, rather than saw, the twist in his mouth as he replied. "The one without a name, I suspect." Then he addressed the spirit control. "Good afternoon. Today I have something different in mind. We are finished with our metaphysical discourses for the time being."

"That is a pity," answered the medium, "for we have only begun."

"There will be other opportunities."

The nameless spirit clucked its tongue. "*Tempus fugit*, Doctor. My compatriot has already warned you of your hourglass. The sand is ebbing."

"Am I to die today? Tomorrow?" the doctor asked, with a cheerfulness that must have astonished the sitters. There was a brief silence. "Ah yes, so there is *some* time left. We shall achieve all things in due course." The doctor opened his portfolio, drew out an envelope and laid it on the table. "Your objective, Sir, is a simple one: to tell us the message contained in this envelope, using words as near verbatim as possible."

From Mrs. Clifford's reply and the murmured conversation that followed, it seemed that Dr. Jennings had devised a new sort of test for her mother's spirit controls. If they were as powerful as they claimed, they ought to be able to read the letter aloud without anyone having to remove it from the envelope.

"Sometimes," Lavinia said dreamily, "when a soul senses its ties to the earth are to be loosened before those of its comrades, it flies in sleep to dwell in the halls of the future. There the spirits of her ancestors may confide in her, and impart to her knowledge which will ease her passage."

It was obvious to Josie that her mother was dallying as if, for the first time ever, she had no idea how to fool them. Dr. Jennings reached forward and tapped his finger on the envelope. "We wish you to tell us the contents of the letter."

There came a long pause, and the word that ended it sent a dart of panic through the girl's heart: "*Josie?*"

The voice came from the medium's chair, but it was

not her mother's voice at all. Josie froze in her crouch on the floor, unable to flee in her terror. *"Josie, are you there?"*

Trembling, she pressed her eye to the keyhole once more, but everyone in their room remained in their chairs. No one knew she was here.

"Josie, where are you?"

She'd never heard it before, and yet she knew beyond all doubt that it was Alec's voice in her mother's mouth. He sounded so forlorn, like he'd been left to wander through some cold gray wasteland beyond the bounds of time. Josie was more frightened for him than she was for herself.

"Josie? . . . Josie!"

Dr. Jennings cleared his throat. "Mrs. Clifford? The contents of the letter, if you will?"

Lavinia drew a ragged breath. "Fatigue. The vessel is weak. I cannot continue. Children of the Infinite, I bid thee Good Day."

Josie gaped. The "spirit," admit failure? This had never happened before!

"The child," Lavinia muttered in her own voice. "The child . . ."

The ladies shifted in their seats, and the first woman leaned over to whisper in the doctor's ear. "What's happening, Dr. Jennings?"

"The child will betray me," Josie's mother said in a cold, calm voice. *"The child will betray me."*

Mrs. Clifford went to bed, taking broth for supper, but when Mr. Berringsley arrived at seven o'clock Merritt carried her down to the reading room sofa. As Josie crept down the stairs in the darkness she heard the key turn in the lock. She pressed her ear to the door.

"Why do you insist upon fretting like an old woman?" her mother said in her ordinary voice. The spirits had worn her out for one day. "I promise you your investments are secure for the time being."

"But how long is 'for the time being'?" Berringsley asked.

"You did not amass such a fortune by second guessing yourself, William, so why must you second guess me now?"

"You did not predict the war." There was a note of petulance in his voice that made Josie smirk. She pressed her hand to her mouth.

Lavinia laughed. "Come now, William! This war is the best thing that ever happened to you. If I'd told you ahead of time you would never have made such appalling sums of money."

The grin melted from Josie's lips. What was it her mother had said at the rally last fall? *The machines of war make men wealthy beyond the grandest imaginings of we ordinary folk.* If Berringsley was one of those men, then that meant her mother had benefited, too—from the very evil she had railed against. "One's choices cannot be made from a place of fear, if one is to succeed," Mrs. Clifford said.

"You are quite right, Lavinia, but you cannot blame me for wanting to secure my legacy. You did say you knew beyond all doubt when the market would crash?"

Her mother sighed. "Not for another twelve years."

"And how did you obtain this information? Was it Baldassare who gave it to you?"

With a curious feeling of serenity Josie waited for the answer. Alec was out of her mother's reach now, and no amount of Mr. Berringsley's money could change that. "I received this particular intelligence through my own hand," said Mrs. Clifford.

How very clever of you, Mother, she thought, her fingers curling into fists. *You have not told a falsehood.*

"May I see the pages?" He thought she meant automatic writing.

"You may not." Mrs. Clifford's reply was brusque. "You are second guessing me again, William. When have I ever given you reason not to trust me?"

Josie rose and went noiselessly up the stairs. Hearing her mother speak of trust made her go cold and shivery, as if she were coming down with the flu.

The Key to the Cupboard
24.

"You got a piece of mail today." Alec's mother held up a small Jiffy envelope. "Who lives on West 87th Street?"

"No idea."

She was skeptical, maybe even a bit worried. "Well, this is for you."

Alec didn't drop his backpack and kick off his shoes as he usually did. He went to his mother, she handed him the package, and he felt around the edges of the object inside (something small and not too heavy, with an irregular shape) before tearing the envelope open. He saw the return address at the top left—*69 West 87th Street, Apt. 29D, New York, NY 10024*—but it meant nothing to him.

Inside the padded envelope was a key, as old and ornate as he thought it would be, and wrapped around the key was a note.

Dear Alec,

Here is the key you've been looking for. I hope someday you can share with me what you find inside.

Very best wishes,
A friend

Mrs. Frost had been reading over his shoulder. The look on her face had gone from worried to frightened. But when Alec ran up the kitchen stairs she was only two steps behind, and she watched from the spare-room doorway as he turned the key in the lock and the tiny door creaked open.

There were two shelves, both of them decked in cobwebs, and from behind these cobwebs shone a pair of bright beady eyes. Mrs. Frost shrieked at first, then began to laugh. "It's a *doll*," she gasped. "Good God, I thought it was a rat."

The shelf was a bit too short for Mrs. Gubbins, so she sat slightly smushed at top and bottom, and on her right by a candy tin rusting around the edges. She had a lace-trimmed cap, one button-eye dangling below the other, a nose shaped with firm stitching out of the fabric of the face, and a long stingy mouth embroidered in what used to be pink. In her letters Josie joked that Mrs. Gubbins was the filthiest doll in the world—*Mrs. Grubbins, more like!*—but Alec smiled to think of how much more dirt she had acquired in the meantime.

Alec reached through the layers of dust and cobwebs and pulled the doll from the shelf. She had dainty hands, the fingers formed with sturdy needle-work in the same manner as the nose, and was surprisingly heavy for a rag doll. *Why did she leave you here?*

"Who sent you the key, Alec? Do you know?" Mrs. Frost went on, almost to herself, "How could *they* know?"

Alec shook his head. "But I know whose doll this is."

She hesitated. "Josephine's little sister?" He nodded. Mrs. Frost sat down heavily on the spare room bed, cradling her forehead in her hand. "I . . ."

"Mom? Are you okay?"

"I don't know how to believe you," she said softly, and when she looked at him there were tears in her eyes.

Alec put the doll back on the shelf. "I don't know what to say, Mom. It's all here. It's *real*."

She held out her arms and he folded himself in. "I'm trying to believe you, sweets." His mother looked at the doll sitting in the cabinet, and the doll looked back. She smiled. "I think I'm almost there."

"I'm sorry I didn't wait for you," Alec said later that evening as he opened the front door for Danny. "I was too excited." There was much more in the cupboard besides Mrs. Gubbins. Together the boys opened the rusted candy tin, and found a sort of time capsule: a postcard from London addressed to "my dearest girls" in extravagant cursive, a deck of cards, a kazoo, and a tiny spinning top, made of metal, with a pointed wooden dowel through the center. He ran his thumb along the words embossed there: *The Famous Confection*. Alec smiled. This had been Cassie's. He'd make it spin on the same floor.

It didn't matter that the postcard was stamped with a date of a hundred and five years before, or that the handful of peppermints no longer looked remotely edible, or that they hadn't spoken through the board in months. Josie had been the last person to touch these things. She felt closer than ever now.

A black cardboard box on the bottom shelf contained a half dozen strange objects, beige and cylindrical. "I'm pretty sure those are wax cylinders," Danny said. "They used to record on them, just for a few years before flat discs got to be standard."

Alec spotted an envelope at the bottom of the box, and it had his name on it in Josie's writing.

My dear friend,

> *These recording cylinders were given to Cass (along with a phonograph) by Mr. Berringsley, who is as convinced as I am that she is destined for the stage. We have observed a series of very curious things about it. While my sister may follow the phonograph instructions to the letter in order to record her elocution exercises, it has not captured her voice at all; no, when we install a cylinder a voice from the future speaks to us, answering all our questions, and we may go on chatting for hours while the cylinder spins, even though wax cylinders are meant to record only two minutes each.*
>
> *Indeed, you and I will speak—yes, speak!— again, and here is what you must do. You must procure a phonograph, though given your connections this will not prove much of a challenge. Load one of these cylinders—any one you choose will be the right one—and listen for us. Danny won't be with you the first time we speak, but do tell him Cass and I look forward to our introduction.*

Your friend,
Josie

"Yeah right I won't be there," Danny said. "I'm not gonna miss this for all the Doritos in Thailand."

The boys resolved to ask Danny's dad for a phonograph after school the next day. It was only later that evening that Alec gave any real thought to the return address, and who "a friend" might be. The handwriting was neat and girlish—not the penmanship of a grown-up—and whoever she was, she maybe spent as much time in Central Park as he had, back when they lived in Manhattan. She was a perfect stranger and yet she knew who he was; she knew about Josie and Cass, and why he needed to open the spare-room cupboard; and she expected that someday they would meet.

So Much Fuss
25.

Lavinia Clifford seldom hosted a party. One's guests had a way of making themselves tedious well before the evening's end, and one couldn't very well dismiss them in contempt when they happened to be one's bread and butter. Besides, parties cost money, and stray bits of hors d'oeuvres mashed into the carpet or between the seat cushions would try Mrs. Pike's patience for days to come.

But Mrs. Clifford's birthday was approaching, and Mr. Berringsley announced that he intended for her a present so marvelous it could only be given at a dinner party in the old French style. They must invite prominent members of the New York Theosophical Society, and serve only the finest champagne and foie gras.

Josie sat at the window watching the guests arrive, Emily's copy of *The Woman in White* splayed on her knee. Cass was busy at the school table, and Josie went over to look at four drawings spread across the desk. "See," said Cass, "this is the big London store with all the animals in their cages, and this is Mr. Berringsley buying the tiger and walking it home to his flat, and here is the tiger sleeping in the bathtub, and here is the tiger getting angry for being kept on the leash and eating Mr. Berringsley for breakfast."

"We'd better make sure Mother doesn't see that one."

"Mrs. Gubbins says you should never try to keep a wild animal. It is a very stupid thing to do, she says."

The sound of another motorcar brought Josie back to the window seat, and she watched an elegant couple stride up to the house with a pang of longing. "It is the ultimate indignity," she sighed as the doorbell rang, "not to be invited to a dinner party under one's own roof."

"Don't be silly." Cass was adding one last flourish to the gory drawing. "You don't care for Mr. Berringsley anyhow."

"Neither do you, apparently!" her sister retorted, and they fell over themselves laughing.

Mrs. Pike brought up their dinner, and when the housekeeper returned for the empty serving tray she said, "You girls are wanted downstairs. Mrs. Clifford is asking for you."

Cass and Josie stood in the doorway of the drawing room, which with all its chatter and sparkle seemed to belong in a different house altogether. The whole of the ground floor was redolent of musky perfumes, pipe smoke, and roasted chicken, and there were many people they did not recognize: sophisticated women in beaded gowns that left their arms quite bare and tall bearded gentlemen in black evening jackets. The upright piano had been moved into the drawing room for the occasion, and a stranger sat playing some exuberant show tune with the nub of a cigarette pinched between his lips. Cass took her sister's hand and squeezed it. They would wait and observe until their mother called upon them.

Someone was speaking, but the voice burbled past her ears like water in a brook. A figure in a wooden mask, painted with three vertical blue stripes on either cheek, sat at the center of a circle of women and men— she recognized the crimson silk dress the figure wore— and Josie realized with a start that it was her mother. The eyes inside the mask moved to meet hers, glittered for a moment, and turned back to the conversation.

"But why should a medium of genuine ability engage in fraudulent acts?" a man was asking as he dropped a pinch of tobacco into his pipe.

"The pressure of performing, of course," said a long-faced woman in a dress of pale blue lace, who seemed to be about their mother's age. "What if, for whatever reason, the spirits remain silent on the day of some visit by a bereaved friend or lover, or a psychical researcher like Dr. Jennings? Does the medium announce to all those assembled that no one is whispering to her today? Certainly not. It would destroy her credibility."

The man lit a match, and it flared as he inserted it into the bowl of his pipe. "Yet she also destroys her credibility through fraudulent acts, the cheesecloth 'ectoplasm' and suchlike."

"Some would argue that it is all for the greater good, Mr. Devers," replied the woman in the blue lace gown.

"She must fall upon her lesser, yet more reliable powers of practical intuition."

"By 'practical intuition,' do you mean her ordinary powers of observation?" asked Mr. Devers as he puffed on his pipe. "The scuff of the boots, the circles under the eyes? In other words, discernment, in its most cynical form? I believe it is called 'cold reading.'"

"I must say I disagree with you, Mrs. Snyder," said Miss Berringsley, who was seated on the other side of Mrs. Clifford. "Fraud and trickery are fraud and trickery, and there can be no excuse for it."

Mrs. Snyder turned to her hostess for the approbation no one else was willing to give her, and Lavinia's mask made it seem as if her guest were bending at the foot of a pagan idol. "I hope you will not take offense, Mrs. Clifford. *You* never cheat, of that I am convinced."

The medium removed the mask from her face, and fixed her cold eyes on the speaker. "Is that so, Mrs. Snyder? How can you be so certain?"

Mrs. Snyder made an attempt at laughter, and the moment seemed on the verge of extending itself intolerably before the pipe-smoking gentleman caught sight of the two figures in the doorway. "The Clifford girls, at last!" he said, and their mother beckoned them into the room.

"Here are my daughters. Say hello, children." Dutifully they obeyed, and Mrs. Clifford rose from her seat and dug her fingernails into Josie's shoulders. "I fill your wardrobe with fashionable frocks, and this is the rag you wear to meet my friends?" she hissed into Josie's ear. Her breath smelled of spirits.

"Mrs. Pike didn't say anything about changing our dresses," Josie whispered back.

"Never mind now." Her mother stood up and cast a

smile around to all in their immediate company. "Miss Berringsley would like to hear you recite something, Josephine."

Josie turned to Mr. Berringsley's sister, who regarded her with one steady eye. "I have only learned a few pieces, ma'am. I could recite 'The Walrus and the Carpenter,' or 'Ozymandias,' or perhaps 'The Charge of the Light Brigade'?" She'd been midway through learning "Goblin Market," but hadn't the heart to continue after Emily's departure.

"*I* could recite something," Cass broke in. "I'm an awfully good actress. Everybody says so."

"Next time, dear," Miss Berringsley replied. "'The Charge of the Light Brigade,' Josephine—that is, if you would be so kind"; and Josie was not as nervous as she might have been, for Miss Berringsley was not the mocking type. A hush fell over the drawing room, and Josie delivered her rendition of Tennyson's poem with only one brief hesitation. It was Emily Jasper's belief that a poem with a plot is far easier to commit to memory, and, in the warmth of that applause, Josie knew then how right she'd been.

As the clapping died away, Mr. Berringsley clinked a spoon against his empty sherry glass. "It's time!" he cried, as one person dimmed the lights, two others carried in a pair of large objects draped in black cloth, and yet another brought in a three-tiered birthday cake on which a multitude of tiny candles danced and flick-ered. "My dear Lavinia! Are you ready?"

"So much fuss!" murmured Mrs. Clifford, but her cheeks glowed with pleasure.

The song was sung and the candles extinguished, but then something very strange happened. From one of the tall black-shrouded objects on the banquet table an inhuman voice squawked, *Alas! He is betrayed and I undone!*

The guests gasped, giggled, or whispered among themselves as Berringsley said, "It seems the cat is out of the bag. Or the birds, as it were." And he drew the black drapes from a pair of gilded cages. "They are Vasa parrots and have come to you all the way from Madagascar by way of London."

Again one of the birds cried out. *Othello! Othello! Forgive me! Othello!*

"Perhaps I should mention," Mr. Berringsley went on, "that they are called Desdemona and Othello."

"Marvelous!" cried Mr. Devers of the ivory pipe. "You're a magician, Berringsley."

"Ah, no," laughed Mr. Berringsley. "I am merely a patient man."

"Those are funny names," said Cassie.

"They're Shakespearean," Josie replied.

Alas! He is betrayed and I undone!

Mr. Berringsley turned to the girls and bowed to meet their faces in his disconcerting way. "Splendid, is it not? I taught her myself."

"Can she say anything else?" Cass asked eagerly.

"She can, if you teach her."

"Can we teach her to talk back to us? Can she answer my questions?"

"I'm afraid not."

"Does Othello know how to talk, too?"

"He does, but he isn't as talkative. You see, Desdemona is the dominant bird."

"Are they brother and sister or husband and wife?" Cassie asked.

"Oh, most certainly husband and wife."

"Then why don't they live in the same cage?"

Mr. Berringsley smiled. "As in any human marriage, it is beneficial that the male and the female spend a certain amount of time apart." Then in a low voice he said something to their mother that Josie did not catch.

Cass was so near Desdemona's cage that the tip of her nose was poking through the thin metal bars. "Say 'Peter Piper picked a peck of pickled peppers.' Go on, Desdemona!"

"Gracious, that's a tricky one even for a smart bird like Desdemona!" laughed Mr. Berringsley.

"That's enough, now," said Mrs. Clifford. "Children, run along up to bed."

"Those parrots have been his precious secret for months," Josie heard Miss Berringsley say as they went out of the room. "Ever since we returned from London, you know. I must confess that we were horribly afraid one of the birds would die before your birthday!"

The girls lay awake, listening to the hum of laughter, piano music, and conversation that went on well into the night.

A Telephone Through Time
26.

Mr. Penhallow frowned. "What can you want with an antique phonograph?"

"Alec found some wax cylinders in that funky cabinet in his house," Danny said, as Alec hurriedly opened the box and pulled out a cylinder to illustrate. "We just want to listen to them. I mean, I guess if you're afraid the phonograph's too fragile, we could just play them here . . .?"

Alec shot his friend a glance, but he relaxed when he saw the look on Danny's face. His dad wouldn't go for that, not with customers in the shop, and Danny knew it.

Mr. Penhallow shook his head and sighed. "If you break it I'm selling your Xbox on eBay and the rest of it's coming out of your allowance 'til you're thirty, you got me?"

Danny grinned. "I got you. We'll be careful, Dad, we promise." Eyeing his browsing customers first to make sure no one was almost ready to check out, Mr. Penhallow ducked into the stock room to find a box for the phonograph.

While they waited, Alec looked around. There were two gramophones in the shop, each with its own cabinet, and only one phonograph, and though there were three shelves of records there were no wax cylinders that he could see.

"Hey, check this out." Danny handed Alec a picture of two young women, sisters, sitting on a hill overlooking a lake. One of the girls was gazing out at the water with a sad look on her face, but there was something odd about the other one. She was sitting slightly tipped forward and her eyes were closed. Like Josie's portrait, this picture was signed and captioned by the photographer. *Penelope & Isabella, 1911.*

"Postmortem photography was totally a thing back then," Danny was saying. "You see how she's got her hand around her sister's waist to keep her up?"

"But they're so *young*," Alec said. The two girls couldn't be more than twenty.

Danny shrugged. "TB, I guess."

Alec suppressed a shudder. There were so many more things a person could die from back then.

He'd washed Mrs. Gubbins's dress, apron, and bonnet in the bathroom sink, wiping her face and hands with a damp cloth, and now she sat on his bookshelf like a new woman—albeit no less mad-looking than when she'd belonged to Cass, since he hadn't yet fixed her dangling button eye. It almost felt as if the doll were supervising them as they set up the phonograph on Alec's desk.

They installed the recording cylinder as Mr. Penhallow had shown them, and when Alec turned on the machine it made a whirring noise as the cylinder spun. A tiny voice came through all the crackling and static, and they strained their ears to listen. *Round and round the rugged rock the ragged rascal ran...*

Danny's phone buzzed, and he groaned as he saw who was calling. "Mom? Please can I just stay a little while longer? . . . but can't I see Aunt Brenda later? She's here all week!" He sighed. "I'm sorry, Mom. I didn't meant to be rude. I'll be home in two minutes." Danny stuffed the phone back in his pocket with a grumpy look.

Alec grinned. "I had a feeling."

Voices on the Phonograph
27.

Josie waited to knock until there was a pause in the clackety-clack of the Royal typewriter.

"Yes?" her mother called. "What is it?" The girl opened the door and went into the room. Her mother rolled her eyes. "Can't you see I'm working?"

"I won't keep you long." Cassie's footsteps skittered down the stairs as she began. "It's been more than three months since you sent Emily away. When will we have a new tutor?"

"When I *find* you a new tutor. Really, Josephine, you can be so tiresome."

From the doorway Cass piped up, "Can't you write to Emily and tell her it was a mistake?"

Mrs. Clifford flashed her younger daughter one of her Looks. "It was not a mistake."

Josie tried again. "Couldn't we go to the day school?"

"And spend your time gossiping with Mabel Foley and her silly friends? I think not."

"They're learning more than I am at the moment." Those precious lively minutes at the birthday party had shown her just how isolated they truly were. They *must* go to school, even if Mabel Foley went on laughing at her, and even if they did not learn any more than they could have at home.

"I sent away for those lectures, and Cassandra finally has her precious elocution exercises," Mrs. Clifford pointed out. "Don't you stand there telling me I won't let you learn anything."

"I can't ask questions from a book of lectures," Josie said. "Besides, it's difficult to concentrate on my reading with Cass always speaking aloud."

"You make me glad all over again for having dismissed Miss Jasper," her mother replied coolly. "You two are the most exasperatingly undisciplined children." Lavinia looked at her younger daughter, and sniffed. "Honestly, some days I can't even tell what Mr. Berringsley sees in you."

Josie cleared her throat. "If all that's true, then isn't it all the more reason to send us to school?"

"You are already aware of my position on that subject." She took a fresh sheet of paper from the stack on her desk and loaded it into the typewriter.

"We can't live like this."

Her mother raised an eyebrow. "Live like what, Josephine?"

"Cooped in this house. You never allow us to go anywhere, not even for a walk in fine weather."

"I do not allow it because I recall what happened the last time you were permitted out of the house on your own."

"You could walk with us," Cass pointed out.

Her mother laughed, as if the idea were patently ridiculous. "*I* have a book to finish."

Josie folded her arms. "You go for walks with Merritt."

"*That*, my dears, is my precious serenity-time, without the likes of you encroaching upon my addled mind—as you are doing now, I might point out."

"This isn't fair!" Josie cried. "We are like two figures in a dollhouse, only making an imitation at living."

"That's very poetic," her mother said dryly as she made a show of looking over the page she'd just finished typing. "Perhaps you should try your hand at free verse. You might become a famous hermit poetess, like Emily Dickinson, and everyone will say how my cruelty inspired your very best work."

"How long are we to go on living like this, Mother? Where shall I go when I am grown? What shall I do? How shall I be of use to anyone outside this house?"

"Heaven knows, as you are precious little use to anyone inside it."

Josie knew she could not pause to contemplate this remark or the hurt would eclipse her resolve. "Will you ever let me leave this house? Will you permit me to go to college, or to marry?"

"You are twelve years of age. So no, I shall not permit you to marry."

Josie's last scrap of dignity finally deserted her. She stamped her foot. "Don't mock me."

"*What* did you say?"

"You are mocking me, Mother. I may be only twelve years of age, but I will not stand to be mocked."

Mrs. Clifford smiled that disdainful smile. "I did not invite you in here to mock you. You invited yourself."

* * *

"Round and round the rugged rock the ragged
rascal ran," Cass said, careful to enunciate each and
every consonant. "Round and round the rugged rock the
ragged rascal ran!"

Josie looked up from her copy of *Brown University's
Lectures in Natural History, Volume One.* "Do you have to
say the same line *quite* so many times?"

"I'm supposed to say each line twelve times before
I go onto the next," Cass replied matter-of-factly. "Mrs.
Gubbins says not to worry if I irritate you now, because
someday you'll be *terribly* proud of me."

Josie rolled her eyes before making another half-
hearted attempt to comprehend the densely-worded
text in front of her. She cradled her chin in her palm,
wondering if anyone would notice or care if she crept
back to her bed at three o'clock in the afternoon.
Then—through the soft rhythmic scratching of the
needle against the lock groove, beneath her sister's
tedious recitations—she thought she heard a voice.

Josie?

She cocked her head this way and that, like a bird.

Cass?

"Shh," Josie said. "Stop for a moment. Do you hear
that?"

Cass stopped speaking, and her eyes went saucer-
wide as the voice came through the phonograph horn
again:

Josie, are you there?

"You're not recording on that cylinder," Josie said
slowly.

The girls paused, waiting. *I can hear you!* said a boy's
voice. *Through the phonograph horn!*

"It's Alec!" Cass cried.

Josie felt her heart thudding against her blouse. "It can't be!"

Josie? Cass? It's me! I'm here!

Cass stuck her head into the phonograph horn. "What are you *doing* in there, Alec?"

They heard him laugh. *You sound just like I thought you would, Cass.*

And Josie knew then, beyond all earthly doubt— since she had already heard Alec's voice once before— that Lavinia Clifford was at least half of what she claimed to be. "How did you ever . . . ?" Josie began faintly. "I never thought I'd speak to you again. And *speak*—truly speak! How have you managed it?"

You wrote me a letter telling me what to do.

Josie frowned. "But I . . ."

You haven't done it yet, but you will. You see? The future you wrote to the me from the past. Doesn't that blow your mind?

"Blow your mind," she murmured. "Yes, I suppose it does." She sighed. "I'm so sorry, Alec. I never should have cooperated with her. I should have known how it would turn out." Again she thought of his voice coming out of her mother's mouth, and shivered. But it *was* the best feeling in the world, to call him by name!

There was nothing you could have done, Josie. He told them about finding Mrs. Gubbins and the "time capsule" box in Emily's old cabinet. *We found these wax cylinders, too, you put them in a box for us, and Danny's dad let us borrow an old phonograph.*

"Did you like the peppermints?" Cass cut in. "The peppermints were *my* idea."

"Hush up and let him speak, will you?"

"We've missed you, Alec," Cass sighed. "I wish we

could hop on a boat and come see you."

You don't have to go anywhere, he pointed out with a laugh. *You can hang tight, but you're going to have to wait awhile.*

"You know something, Alec?" said Cass. "You talk kind of peculiar."

Josie nudged her sister. "Don't be rude!"

It's okay. You guys talk a bit strange too. It's the time difference. He laughed.

They talked for two hours that first afternoon: of Emily's dismissal, and their inability even to go for a walk around the block, and of Alec running out on his dad to watch these things called robots—*like mechanical people*—sing Christmas carols instead. At one point Josie instructed him to go on talking about nothing important until she told him he could stop, and she went out into the corridor and closed the door. "I couldn't hear you from outside," she said when she came back in. "That means we can talk to you all we like and no one will know."

Mrs. Pike rang the bell for dinner, and they reluctantly said their goodbyes. Josie clasped her sister by the shoulders. "You must promise not to say a word about this to anyone. And by 'anyone,' I mean Mother *especially*."

That night they talked again, fielding Cassie's frequent interjections. "What do you look like, Alec? Are you tall or small? Stout or lean?"

"Cass!" Josie gasped. "It isn't polite to ask someone if they're stout!"

"Brown hair or blond?" she went on. "Green eyes or blue? Do you have freckles across your nose? I have a freckle on my nose, and I named it Esmeralda."

At last the little girl wore herself out. Josie carried

her to bed, and turned back to the phonograph. "Could you see me?" She hesitated. "In your time?"

You'd love it here, Josie. Women can do anything they want to.

"Of course you know we can't vote. It's the one thing Mother and I agree on."

You will, he said. *I looked it up. Women in New York State get to vote in 1917. That's only next year. And in 1920 there'll be a constitutional amendment. Then every woman in America will be able to vote.*

"1920 feels like a lifetime from now," she said. "I wish I could live in the future. Life must be so much easier and *fairer* then."

It's definitely not perfect. We're making a mess of the planet, and a lot of rotten stuff has happened. Stuff I didn't tell you much about when your mom took over the board.

"You mean the wars?"

And lots of other stuff you don't need to know about. He paused. *It's not like you could do anything about it.*

"You don't think we can change what's to come?"

Not the big stuff, I don't think. But maybe we can make a difference to each other.

"You already have," she said softly. "Oh, Alec. It is so good to know the sound of your voice."

How about this? If you could go anywhere in time . . .

"Besides twenty-sixteen, you mean?"

She could hear the smile in his voice. *Yeah. If you could only go backwards.*

"I'd go to the library at Alexandria." She paused, considering. "Of course, I'd have to study all the old languages before I went, so I could actually read the parchments."

Talking to Alec through the phonograph was the best sort of secret: it hurt no one to keep it, and it made their lonely days much easier to live through. It was like a butterscotch candy that never melted.

CLIFFORD

Afraid of the Truth
28.

Grammy Sal came and baked enough snickerdoo-
dles to satisfy every sweet tooth in Edwardstown. Alec
was happy to see her—not to mention grateful for the
treats—but the reason for her visit weighted every lull
in the conversation. While he was in school they were
going into the city so his mother could sign the divorce
papers.

Late that night he went down the back stairs for a
cookie before he settled in to talk to Josie and stopped
just out of sight when he heard his mother crying.
She was trying to speak, but she was so upset that he
couldn't make out any words. "Shh, shh," murmured
Grammy Sal. "I know, honey. I know he did. And there
isn't a doubt in my mind that, at the time, he meant it."

I'm sorry about your parents, Josie said.
He thought back over the end of last summer, how

everything had haunted him then, and how it felt as if it always would. "It's okay. I mean, not *okay*, but it could be worse, right?"

There was a silence on the other end of the phonograph, and he began to wonder if he'd put his foot in it. When Josie spoke again she changed the subject. *I wish I knew how to bake. Mrs. Dowd will never let me make anything. Sometimes I feel that I'll be stuck in this house forever—always a nuisance, always a child.*

"It won't always be like that." Alec spoke with more certainty than he felt. Logically he knew that they would both grow up, leave this house, and do whatever they wanted—or at least that was what they were *meant* to do. The tiny gravestone nudged itself back into his thoughts.

Danny had been desperate for a sleepover, but Grammy Sal's visit had prevented it. Now that he'd finally gotten his opportunity to talk to the Clifford girls, Alec had never seen him so exuberant. The present-day bedroom could not contain his energy, and it flowed through the phonograph horn, where Cass picked it up on the other end and giggled uncontrollably. *Don't mind her,* Josie said. *She's laughing at her own farts again.*

"Wait," said Danny. "You say 'fart'?"

Why, what other word would I use?

"I guess I thought it was a new word."

Alec felt a flicker of frustration that they couldn't talk about more important things with Danny here, but then, it didn't seem fair to be irritated with Danny either. He made an effort to laugh when they did.

As the conversation continued, with Danny gleefully egging Cass on ("a snot-rocket is when you blow your nose, and it hangs down to your chin all yellow and goopy"), Alec could hear Josie's embarrassment for having to hush her sister. *You'll think I really am the most horrible scold, Danny, but we can't risk anyone coming in here and discovering this.*

"Sorry, Josie," said Danny, making an attempt to sober himself. "I wouldn't want to get you guys in trouble. Alec told me how it ended last time."

"Dude, that was the weirdest, awesomest thing that ever happened to me," he murmured from the spare room once the girls had said their goodbyes. They'd left the adjoining door open at bedtime so they could talk. "My dad's starting to ask when we're giving back the phonograph, but don't worry, I'll put him off for as long as I can."

The graveyard was a different place by day. The breeze blew through the sycamores, making the leaves shiver audibly. Rabbits and squirrels, robins and sparrows and even a bluejay hopped between the headstones. The whole place smelled fresh and green and new.

In daylight they could also see the stained glass windows inside the mausoleums. They paused at one, marked BERRINGSLEY in the stone above the doorway, and pressed their faces against the elaborate wrought-iron gate. There were dead leaves and animal droppings all over the marble floor. "Doesn't matter how much money you got," Danny remarked. "You're still gonna die, and birds are gonna poop all over you."

For a while they wandered around the tiny gray buildings and took in the view over Edwardstown, all the Victorian rooftops, tidy streets and towering maples. They'd come to look at the grave again, but, now that they were here, Alec dreaded the sight of it.

Then suddenly it was right in front of them, the mottled little marker a stark reminder of all the things he could not change. In the dark that Halloween night he hadn't noticed the weeping angel just beyond the tiny grave. *WILLIAM CLIFFORD*. "Cassie's father," Alec said, pointing. His was the only name on the headstone.

Danny took out his phone and snapped a picture. "Whose do you think the little one is?"

"I'm afraid to find out."

"Alec," Danny said, and he knew what his friend was going to say. "It might be hers, or it might be someone else's, but it doesn't change—"

"I know. I *know* she's dead." He didn't want to think of either of them lying here under the grass. They didn't belong here, not when he'd heard their laughter the night before, his name in their mouths. "I know they're gone," he managed to say. "But I can still worry about how and when, can't I? It still matters." He sat cross-legged in the grass, his elbows on his knees, his fist against his cheek.

Danny plopped down beside him. "Maybe it's Lavinia's."

"No way. She would've had a huge stone with a whole flock of sobbing angels." Alec sighed. "Every other stone that size belongs to a kid."

The next day they went to the library and sat down at the terminals. "We should find out if they have any descendants," Danny said. "Maybe there are some still living here."

It was downright weird to think of Josie and Cassie having children and grandchildren, but he needed to know. Alec input the search terms—*Clifford, Josephine, 1915-1930*—and held his breath.

The results went on for pages. *Clifford, Josephine, author. New York Evening Star.* The dates ranged from 1921 to 1930. "She's a journalist!" He was dizzy with delight. He couldn't wait to tell her. *The grave,* he thought. *It can't be hers.*

"Print, print, print!" Danny chanted, and Alec printed out the first few articles in the list to read later.

"Now for Cassie." This time he tried a wider date range, since Cassie was younger, but there were no hits for *Clifford, Cassandra, Clifford, Cassie,* or *Clifford, Cass.*

"What if you widen the date range?"

Alec shook his head. It was like this: if he were to find out exactly where, when, and how, then he wouldn't be able to change it.

Instead Danny typed in *Lavinia Clifford, obituary.* "Wow. She was pretty young."

Alec craned his neck. "How young?"

"Forty-five." The medium had died, so it said, of a nervous illness brought on by the stress of her calling. It was a condensed version of the profile they'd read in the Spiritualist magazine, mentioning Horace Vande-grift and William Berringsley, and even the name of her bodyguard. Alec read it over two more times, as if the words could change to tell him what he needed to know. Why wasn't there any mention of Lavinia Clif-ford's daughters?

"That's weird. The obit always lists children, doesn't it?" Danny muttered, as if reading his thoughts.

"There's something else we should check." Alec

opened a new window and Googled *child abuse laws history*. He clicked on the first link and the boys read the article together. The first federal child protection laws weren't passed until 1974, it read, although there were independent welfare agencies from the 19th century onward. The New York Society for the Prevention of Cruelty to Children was founded in 1875. Not much, but better than nothing.

Outside again, Danny paused at the town hall entrance. "I bet they have the cemetery records here, too. We could find out right now." Alec shook his head. "We have to, dude. I'll just run in." Danny disappeared inside and he paced the sidewalk. This was it—or at least it might be.

A couple minutes later he'd just decided to follow him in when Danny reappeared. "No good," he said. "The lady at the front desk says the land belongs to the township now, so the records are definitely upstairs, but I went up there and nobody's around."

When Alec sighed, it was mostly with relief. Whatever the truth was, they wouldn't find it today.

The End of the Future
29.

Every night they looked forward to bedtime, when the harsh words and long silences of the day were behind them, and they could speak to their friend from the future. Now that they were at liberty to communicate every night, their respective timelines seemed to realign themselves, so tomorrow for Alec was no longer two weeks later for Josie.

Once Cass was asleep Josie would turn back to the phonograph with a smile no one could see, for now they were free to talk of anything they wanted. Tonight, in particular, she felt Alec was waiting to tell her about something more important than motorcars powered by the rays of the sun, or typewriters that could tell you anything you needed to know.

Is Cassie asleep?

Her sister slept with her arms clenching her pillow and her eyes shut tight, as if she were bracing herself for a plunge. Josie thought of the Lusitania, and the Titanic, and shivered. "Yes," she whispered. "She's asleep."

I have two things to tell you. Important things. He paused. *I found you in the newspaper.*

"Oh dear." She tried to laugh, but her heart was thudding.

Alec laughed too. *Not like that. You're a journalist. I wish I could show you these articles! You've written lots of interesting stuff—there's a piece about a speakeasy in the Village getting shut down by the police, and the other one I have here is an interview with a poet who won the Pulitzer Prize. He told you he only writes in the bathtub.*

She felt the goose-pimples rising on her arms, but the strangest part of her reaction was this: she wanted to cry.

Josie? Are you there?

"Yes," she whispered. "I suppose I need a moment to take it in."

I bet! If somebody told me for sure what I'd be doing in ten years, I know I'd be freaked out.

"'Freaked out,'" she murmured. "I can guess what that means."

But you're glad I told you, right?

"Of course, Alec!" She thought of what Cassie had said the night of the rally. *I could sit back and look forward to it all.* "It's such a gift, and I don't know how to thank you."

Nah. You'd have done the same for me.

"What was the other thing you wanted to tell me?"

She felt a chill blow clear through her at what he said next. *It's hard for me to talk about it, Josie. We could say . . . it's the end of the future.*

"I see," she said finally. Now her heart was pounding so loudly she wondered if Alec could hear it too. Did she want to know?

Yes—yes. He wouldn't have brought it up if it weren't something he thought could be changed. "Tell me," she said, and listened as he drew a deep breath.

There's a stone . . . in the old cemetery on the hill. It . . . it . . .

"Whose name is on it?" she asked, all foreknowledge of her future life in print forgotten in an instant, dreading what felt like the inevitable answer: *Yours.*

It just says "Clifford."

She put her hand to her heart. She'd never known there could be such comfort in uncertainty. "It isn't Father Clifford's stone? He is buried there, on the hill, under a weeping angel."

No, it's a very plain marker. It looks like it's a hundred years old. And Josie . . . this is the thing that scares me. It's so small. It only says "Clifford" because there isn't room for anything else.

Her stomach lurched. "No dates?"

No dates. There are other stones that small, but they're always—he hesitated. *They belong to babies.* Another pause. *Kids.*

"Mother once told us there are no other Cliffords in Edwardstown."

The graveyard isn't used anymore. I know the records are kept at town hall, but . . . well, I guess I'm afraid to ask. I just keep thinking about the horrible things your mom does, acting like they're fair punishments. I told you, nobody would be allowed to do that to their kid now. Their children would be taken away from them.

"Yes, but where do they go? Who takes them in?"

Other relatives—nice ones—or foster parents, if they don't have any other family.

"But it isn't that way yet."

Still, there are people who could help you. I've been reading about child protection laws. There were all these cases where children were taken away from their parents because they were shut in closets or basements, or beat up, or not allowed to go to school. I'm telling you, Josie. You have to find a way to contact the New York Society for the Prevention of Cruelty to Children.

"There's no way I could do that. And even if I could . . . where would we go? How would we live?" she asked, even as a tiny voice in her head said, *Emily. Find Emily.*

I don't want to tell you what to do, but . . . I'm afraid for you, Josie. I keep thinking maybe this is why . . . why . . .

Why they were given this chance, he meant—this bridge across the century. She didn't know what to say. More than ever she wanted to reach through the mouth of the phonograph and take her friend by the hand.

Just think about it, all right?

"I will. I'll think about it." She hesitated. "Alec . . . there's something I've been wanting to ask you for a long time."

I know what you're going to say, but I . . .

"Have you found it?" She couldn't seem to lift her voice above a whisper. "Do you know when I . . . ?"

No! he said, with a fierceness that clutched at her heart. *I don't—I never looked for it—and I don't ever want to talk about you being dead. I don't think of you that way. I'll never think of you that way. You're the same age as me, and you're my friend.*

Her tears fell without sniffles or sobs—she *wanted* to cry, but she could not wake Cass—and yet he seemed to know. *I'd give anything*, he said, *to hand you a tissue.*

Some days the nursery walls seemed to draw in on them, and they seized upon any excuse to venture downstairs. On those occasions Cass invariably got herself into mischief, and thus a simple scavenging for a sandwich would end in a nasty scolding.

One overcast afternoon, having learned from their mistakes of late, they went up to the attic. The room was empty apart from a few pieces of furniture Mrs. Clifford had already decided to replace, and they found it peaceful to stand at the windows overlooking the backyard and watch as the sky went yellow like an old photograph. It began to rain, and Josie pulled up the sashes to let in the cool damp air. She breathed it in, closed her eyes, and imagined for a moment that she was scything her way through the jungle.

She carried a cane chair into the light—what little there was that day—and opened her book as Cassie fell into a waltz step around the empty room, giggling to herself and holding Mrs. Gubbins as if the doll were her partner.

An hour slipped by as Josie lost herself in her book. *The Weir of Hermiston* was another novel Emily left behind, and her tutor had told her—how long ago it seemed, that happy afternoon of her arrival, when they'd sat on her bed swinging their legs as she unpacked her books!—that Stevenson had died before he could complete it. It was the story of a boy whose father showed him no love, no affection, and it cut too true to put down.

A scratching noise drew Josie out of the story. Cass was bent over the windowsill at the far end, her elbow working in and out like a bellows. "Cass? What are you doing over there?" The little girl made no answer, and Josie laid down her book and went over.

With a long nail she must have found on the floor, Cass had scratched HELLO into the windowsill, and was almost finished carving Alec's name.

Josie stared, mouth agape. The night Alec had told her of the message in the windowsill Cassie had been upstairs asleep, and she could not recall ever telling her about it. "Whatever possessed you to do such a thing?" Cass finished the C and laid down the nail with a shrug. "You couldn't have known," Josie said. "You couldn't have!"

Cassie flashed her impish little grin. "Couldn't have known what?"

Josie shook her head. Everything was happening precisely as it was meant to—where he found a flower, they must plant the seed—and she began to suspect some hidden magic even if Dr. Jennings could someday explain it with textbook precision.

Songs and Stories
30.

Neither of them went as far as to admit it, but if Mrs. Clifford hadn't commandeered the talking board they'd have never discovered the phonograph. Now they got to talk every night, actually *talk* to one another, and for as long as they liked. They heard every sigh and hesitation, every comma, contraction, and exclamation point. They marveled at the strangeness in each other's voices; the way Josie spoke was so crisp, so *correct* compared to the way girls talked at school. He downloaded a voice recorder app and laid his iPod on the table beside the phonograph, although he couldn't have explained why.

He was glad, too, for Cassie's frequent interjections—*do they still have rats and midges in twenty-six-teen, Alec? Is it true the train only takes a day and a half to get from here to San Francisco? There's a porch swing? I wish we had a porch swing!*—even though he could hear how they aggravated her sister. They would wait until the little girl fell into bed before continuing in hushed voices. He described the Little Free Library on the corner of Falcon and Juniper, and *The Nightmare Before Christmas*, and the three-dimensional cake shaped like a yellow Volkswagen Beetle his mother baked from scratch for his ninth birthday. He told her about the moon landing, and the Civil Rights movement, and the first African-American president, and how Pluto had once been a planet but wasn't anymore. *If you are traveling in space*, she asked, *sooner or later won't you collide with a star?*

"I don't think so. The stars are much farther away than they look."

He read whole books to her that hadn't been written yet: *The Phantom Tollbooth*, *The Chronicles of Narnia*, and *Coraline*, which he realized too late had made her uneasy. *From now on I shall always picture my mother with buttons for eyes.*

Sometimes he became self-conscious for having spoken so long uninterrupted, because he wanted his friend to know how much he preferred the sound of her voice to his own. But she encouraged him to speak, to tell stories from school or of his old life in Manhattan, and to go on reading even when he knew she must be falling asleep.

One night in May, Alec set up his iPod and speakers ("it's like a gramophone," he said, "except it's the size of a very small book and all the records are inside") and played her some of his favorite songs. "What do you think?"

It took her a moment to answer. *It's quite . . . strange, isn't it?*

"Of course it's strange," he laughed. "It's called rock music. It hasn't been invented yet."

They talked until they found themselves forgetting what they had heard or said a moment earlier, and they each accused each other of nodding off, though, of course, they were equally guilty.

Something began to feel different. He watched his mom making plans for a future without his dad, walking to the yoga studio on Main Street on weekend mornings, and occasionally heating him up a tin of veggie chili before going out to dinner with new friends, and it was as if he'd let his hands fall from his eyes, let them open. Being afraid for Josie and her sister wasn't the same thing as helping them. So in the end, Danny didn't have to drag him back to town hall.

The foyer smelled of disinfectant and the microwaved leftovers of somebody's tuna noodle casserole. "Room 213, right?" his friend asked the secretary at the front desk, who nodded and pointed to the stairs.

They jogged up the pea-green linoleum steps to the second floor and found the woman behind the desk in room 213 to be the very embodiment of their worst-case scenario. "It would be *impossible* to dig out those records right now," she sniffed. "You do realize it's nearly four o'clock?"

Now that they were finally here, it was unthinkable to have to leave again without finding what they needed. "What if we come back first thing tomorrow?" Alec asked.

The secretary shuffled some papers on her desk. "That depends. What is it for?"

"A summer project on Edwardstown history," Danny replied quickly. "We're researching some of the local suffragists, and our teacher wants us to find out where they're buried."

Alec suppressed a smile. It wasn't precisely the truth, but this *was* a project, and it was much more important than an ordinary school assignment.

"Leave me your name and telephone number along with the names you're looking for," she said, "and I'll have the clerk locate the records you need. I'm just letting you know, it may take him several days to get to it. He's only here part time."

"What if it takes weeks?" Alec sighed as they went down the dingy stairwell.

"Nah." Danny hopped up on the banister and slid down the last few steps, and the secretary at the front desk shot him a stern look. "You gotta follow up with these people or nothing'll ever happen. Let's go back in the morning and see if we can talk to that guy."

THIS TICKET ENTITLES THE BEARER TO ONE VERY SPECIAL SONG FOLLOWED BY A VERY SPECIAL BEDTIME STORY, FROM THE TWENTY-FIRST CENTURY.

The Worst Birthday Ever
31.

The night before Cassie's birthday, she'd been so excited that Josie asked her three times to get back into bed. Now, what ought to have been the most festive of mornings was instead cold and subdued. Her sister came to the breakfast table with a light in her eyes— after all, the whole *world* knew she was seven today, and if they didn't, well, they'd soon find out!—but with each moment that passed in silence, each remark their mother made that was not a felicitation, the light in her eyes dimmed by one degree. By the end of the meal the disappointment was plain on her face, and the sight of it wrung Josie's heart.

Then the little girl—not so little, as of today!— could withstand the suspense no longer. "Mother?"

"Yes, Cassandra?"

"Am I to have a cake tonight?"

"Oh. I suppose it *is* your birthday."

"May I have a chocolate cake? With buttercream icing?"

Her mother opened her mouth to answer, but she was interrupted by a shriek from an adjoining room. "Mrs. Clifford!" cried the housekeeper. "Oh—oh—Mrs. Clifford!"

"What is it, Mrs. Pike?"

"I—oh!—in the drawing room—the parrot, it's . . . it's . . ."

"For heaven's sake!" Mrs. Clifford tossed her napkin onto her plate, and the girls heard her heels go clipping briskly down the corridor. Then there was a long silence.

Josie got up and hurried out of the dining room. Her mother was standing before the birdcages, and as she approached she saw that the cage on the left was empty.

One bird lay on the floor of the other cage in a bloodied heap of feathers, as if it had been mauled by a wild animal. That was impossible, of course, and at first Josie did not understand what had happened. Then she noticed that the head of Othello had been completely severed from his body, and her hand flew to her mouth.

Desdemona stood silently on the perch above her dead mate, lifting her claws and setting them down again to grip the roosting branch. It seemed to be the birdly equivalent of fidgeting in one's seat. Josie glanced at her mother. By now she knew this look all too well.

"Did you do this?"

"*No*, Mother!"

Mrs. Clifford threw up her hands in exasperation. "I didn't mean did *you* eat the parrot, Josephine! Who put them in the same cage?"

Josie paled. So *this* was what Cass had been doing out of bed last night.

"She was so lonely," came a small voice from the drawing room threshold. "Mr. Berringsley said they were married, and I thought . . . I just thought they ought to be together."

"Come here, Cassandra."

But Cass backed away from the door, and their mother hissed, "I said, *come here*, Cassandra. Come here and see what you've done."

Cass came in. Mrs. Clifford pointed to what was left of Othello, and pulled the little girl's hand away when she tried to shield her own eyes. "This, *my dear*, is what occurs when you place the parrots in the same cage without supervision. They are only let into the same cage to breed. Otherwise the female will eat the male. Clearly you were not listening when Mr. Berringsley warned us of this."

"I didn't hear . . . I didn't know . . ." Cass said weakly.

"Of course you didn't. You revel in your ignorance, child. Now you see what comes of being so utterly impulsive—so utterly selfish! What on earth will I tell Mr. Berringsley?"

Cass hung her head. "I don't know."

The cannibal bird opened its beak, and when it spoke the girls started in alarm. *Alas! He is betrayed and I undone!*

"Do you have *any* idea how much Mr. Berringsley paid for that bird?" Mrs. Clifford grasped her daughter by the ear, and Cass cried out. She punctuated each white-hot word with a yank of the little girl's earlobe. "*Do—you—have—any—idea—how—much—Mr.— Berringsley—paid—for— that—bird?*"

"I'm sorry!" Cass was shrieking as she brought up her hands and fumbled against her mother's grip, trying in vain to free her ear. "I'm sorry! I never meant for it to happen!"

"Mother, please!" Josie laid a hand on her mother's arm, but Mrs. Clifford shook her off, giving Cass a right hard slap on her other ear. A trickle of blood went slowly down her sister's neck as Desdemona chirped, *Othello! Othello! Forgive me! Othello!*

At last Mrs. Clifford let go, and Cass buried her face in Josie's chest. Josie pressed a handkerchief to one ear, and then the other, for the ear that had been pulled on was bleeding, too. Their mother sat at the piano, laid her elbow on the fallboard, and cradled her forehead in her hand. "You children will be the death of me," she said. "Now get out. I don't want to see you again today. Mrs. Pike will bring up your meals."

"But it's my birthday," Cassie sobbed.

At this Mrs. Clifford seemed to cast aside her weariness. She let out a hard little laugh. "Have you heard a word I've said, Cassandra? Do you actually believe yourself worthy of a cake? Of presents? Shall I invite Mr. Berringsley and serve his decapitated bird on a silver platter?"

"It's not fair! I didn't know she would eat him!"

Josie watched her mother's face, how a knot formed at her jaw as she clenched her teeth. She rose from the piano bench, stepped toward Cass, and slapped her one last time. "I could *kill* you," she whispered. "I could wring your neck."

That night Josie made her sister a red paper crown. Alec played "happy birthday" through the phonograph with the kazoo from the time capsule. *Where's the box, Cass?* he asked. *Get your kazoo and let's play a duet!*

Josie hadn't been able to buy a present for Cass, so she was obliged to use her imagination. *This ticket entitles the bearer to one very special song, followed by a very special bedtime story, from the twenty-first century.* It was essentially a present from Alec, but she couldn't very well put a book or a hair ribbon in a box and pretend she'd found it in a shop.

For the first part of her gift, Alec plugged his "iPod" into his "speakers" and played a song called "Life in Technicolor." It was strange music, marvelous music, and, in a few minutes, it built a room in their minds that they could live inside.

They heard the smile in Alec's voice. *Now you're the only people in the whole world who've ever heard a Coldplay song.*

"You should see the look on her face," Josie whispered into the horn. "This very nearly makes up for everything that's happened today."

What happened? he whispered back.

She sighed. "I'll tell you later."

"Alec, what's technicolor?" Cass piped up.

Have you ever seen a movie? A film, I mean? A "moving picture"?

"Uh huh. Mr. Berringsley took us once, in New York."

And it was in black and white?

"Of course," Josie replied. "Do you mean to say . . . ?"

Technicolor is even brighter than colors in real life. You'll see. There'll be a movie of The Wizard of Oz.

"Emily read us *The Wonderful Wizard of Oz*," Cass said. "How long must we wait for the film?"

Let me look it up. There was a pause, and Josie knew Alec was using his Times Machine. *About twenty-three years.*

"Why, I'll have grandchildren by then!"

He laughed. *It's not <u>that</u> long!*

"Now it's time for my bedtime story. I would like one about an airship. Have you ever flown into the sunset, Alec? That's what I'm going to do someday when it's the future, and I have my very own aeroplane."

I know just which story to read to you. It's twentieth century, but it hasn't been written yet. So he read from *The Little Prince,* and when she began to nod off he promised to finish the story the following night.

Once Cass was in bed, Josie recounted the events of the morning.

This is terrible, Josie. Have you thought any more about what I said?

"Yes, but . . ."

What about Emily?

"Even if I could write her a letter, how would I put it in the post? Mother would never allow it. I can always tell when we've had a letter from Emily because she takes it out of the stack and hides it away, and doesn't answer when we ask her who it's from."

Do you have any other family?

"None," she sighed. "At least, none that I know of."

Then it's gotta be Emily. You'll reach her. You have to.

She hesitated. "Do you know that for certain?"

I wish I could say yes.

"I can't, Alec. There's no way."

There has to be a way. You said her aunt and uncle live in the city, right?

"That's right."

And didn't you say they're the ones who raised her? So she's probably gone back to live with them, and even if she hasn't, you can at least write to her uncle, and he'll forward her the letter.

"That's true. I could write to him at the *Evening Star*. He's the editor in chief. But how will I ever get a letter out of the house?"

Is there anyone else who could help you? Someone you could write to without making your mother suspicious?

"I don't think so..."

Think!

Then the answer came to her. "Dr. Jennings!" If she could only manage to write to him, he would certainly help her. "He told Mother he'd send her a copy of the first article! Perhaps she'll allow me to write him a thank you."

Yes! You can slip another letter in along with it, and tell him why you can't write to Emily yourself.

"But . . . Alec . . ." Fear bound her hands together. Doubts tore at her insides. "Even if Emily takes us back to the city with her, there remains the question of our keep. I can't possibly expect her to—"

It'll be okay, Josie. You'll find a way. I know you can do it.

They bid each other goodnight, and she climbed into bed, blinking back tears as images welled up out of the darkness: the letters *E.A.J.* in gold leaf, glinting on the lid of the steamer trunk—her mother's eyes glittering through the spirit mask—Merritt's cold white hands grasping Cassie by the waist—the headless bird—the tiny grave.

Josie turned her head and saw Cassie curled up at the head of the bed like a kitten and breathing just as softly. Her doll sat at the foot, nestled in the folds of the quilt.

She'd always reckoned that when Mrs. Gubbins "spoke," it was merely Cassie giving voice to the things she wouldn't otherwise be permitted to say. Mrs.

Gubbins was Cassie's imaginary friend—or imaginary biddy—nothing more than a figment of her own fertile mind. The doll could have no opinion on the fact that she was destined to pass the next hundred years locked inside the spare-room cupboard.

That night Josie tossed and turned under the weight of all her fears and frustrations, and when she did at last drift off, she dreamed she was still awake.

Again she glanced over at Cassie asleep in her narrow bed. Her sister was still slumbering peacefully, but something was different. The doll at the foot of the bed was *staring* at her.

You promised you would look after her. The voice was low but clear, and it sounded for all the world like a woman sixty years of age.

"I'm trying," said Josie.

The doll's face was as stiff and expressionless as ever, yet the voice went on. *You can do better than to try, child, for to try is to fail. Do you see?* The doll was chiding her, but gently, as if it understood the difficulties she faced.

"Then what would you have me do?"

Protect her, said Mrs. Gubbins. *Do as you promised.*

You Never Know
32.

The next morning Danny came by, and they walked into town together. "I guess you haven't heard yet about Harold," Danny said.

Alec raised an eyebrow. "No . . . ?"

"Mrs. Grogan caught him looking through her testing binder at recess the day before the math final. I heard my mom talking to Mrs. Yates about it last night. He's in *deep poop*." Danny shook his head. "He could have gotten an A without cheating. That's the sad thing."

Now that Alec knew what Cassie's voice sounded like, he could imagine exactly how she'd said it: *Mrs. Gubbins says Alec doesn't keep any secrets worth telling. But YOU do . . .*

"You gotta feel for him, though," Danny went on. "If he doesn't get into Harvard, Dr. Yates will pretty much disown him."

"I didn't know his dad was like that," Alec said slowly. If Harold hadn't been a good friend to him, maybe now he could halfway understand why.

When they got to town hall they found the impatient secretary blessedly absent. The boys explained what they needed to a white-haired man in a short-sleeved dress shirt and suspenders who turned out to be the historical records clerk. Danny showed him the photos of the grave he'd taken with his phone.

"I haven't been up there in years," said the clerk, "but that looks like the newest section of the graveyard . . ." The boys exchanged a look—*newest!*—and the man smiled. "Well, it *was* founded in 1797. That stone is early twentieth century. Probably one of the last interments." He pointed through a doorway, where they could see rows of metal shelving crammed with old files and boxes. "We've got the cemetery map with all the plots numbered and indexed, but it may take me a little while to find it. Can you boys come back after lunch?"

They passed the wait at the library. In the archive room, Bernice had left the Clifford box on a low shelf, and Alec pulled out the scrapbook with a sigh. "I don't know why I'm even looking at this again. We've already been through it three times."

Danny shrugged as he shuffled through Lavinia Clifford's correspondence file. "You never know."

Slowly Alec turned the familiar pages of pictures and newspaper clippings. He came to the end of the album, and ran his finger over a tiny nub of paper sticking out from between the leather cover and the black cardboard backing. Carefully, very carefully, he began to pick at the seam. His friend did a silent dance of glee as the square of black cardboard backing came away, leaving a shallow space under the back cover. Alec pulled out a small cache of pictures and papers concealed inside, one of which was a theater program.

Cassandra Jasper in THE COMET PARTY
Written and directed by Byron Grimsby
At The Century Theater
Limited engagement!

Alec stared at the lovely young woman on the play-bill cover. "That's her! That's Cassie! You know what this means?" He jumped up and down in his seat. "The grave can't be hers either!" The boys looked at each other. If they hadn't been in the library they'd have whooped and hollered.

"I saw a picture of a comet party in the shop once," Danny said. "People had these wild-'n-crazy shindigs in 1910 where they'd go up on the roof and drink champagne and watch Halley's Comet go by. Jasper, that's Emily's last name, right? Now we know why we couldn't find anything."

They're going to adopt her, Alec thought. *They'll adopt them both.*

There was a dramatic shadowy studio portrait of Cass, like all the famous old movie stars had, and two informal pictures of the sisters—Josie beaming with pride, Cass holding a bouquet of roses, and figures in motion all around them. These must have been taken right after a performance. Alec looked at the playbill in his hands, feeling dizzy with relief.

When they returned to room 213 the clerk ushered them to a big, yellowed map spread out over a desk, the curling edges weighted down with moldy-smelling hardcovers. "First I found the plot on the map"—he pointed to a tiny block on the grid—"and then I looked up the number in the ledger-book. The grave you're interested in isn't quite as old as it looks—it dates to 1927. As a matter of fact, it was the very last interment at Mount Hope." He turned the ledger around so they could read it, and pointed. Alec leaned in for the name under the clerk's fingertip, and it was just as he'd expected: *Clifford, Lavinia.*

Her Fate in Her Hands
33.

"Cass?"

"Mmm-hmm?"

"When Mrs. Gubbins speaks to you . . ."

Cassie looked up from her drawing and cocked her head.

"Do you see her lips move, or is it as if a voice is talking in your mind?"

"Her lips don't move, silly. She's a *doll*."

"So it *is* like a voice speaking in your mind?"

Her sister shrugged. "I don't know. I never thought of it that way."

"The next time she speaks to you, will you try to notice?"

"Why?"

"Because I need to know."

"But why?" Cass stared at her sister. "Did she talk to you, too?"

"I don't know."

"Mrs. Gubbins says she talks to me because I listen. That's why she's my friend. She says there's no point talking to folks if they don't want to hear what you have to say. It's very fusterating. She says most people are deaf even though their ears work just fine."

"Cass . . . who *is* Mrs. Gubbins? And how does she know things?"

Cassie shrugged.

"I mean it. I want to know. How did she know that you'll be married someday, but I won't?"

The little girl shook her head. "She said she would never have told me that if she'd known I was going to gab about it. You weren't supposed to know. It was meant to be a secret."

Josie tried again and again, but Cass wouldn't tell her anything else. Evidently she had learned her lesson too well.

A parcel arrived in the mail, and Mrs. Clifford opened it over luncheon. It was the latest edition of *The Proceedings of the American Society for Psychical Research*, with an article entitled "Mrs. Lavinia Clifford: A Case Study in Telepathy" bookmarked with Dr. Jennings's business card. The enclosed note was written in the doctor's own hand:

My dear Mrs. Clifford:

*Here is the first of several articles I intend to
publish on the nature of your extraordinary ability.
I shall forward the others in due time.*

Sincerely yours,
Henry Jennings

Josie read the note while her mother skimmed the
article. Judging by her reaction, Dr. Jennings hadn't
written the fawning analysis Mrs. Clifford had been
expecting. "Rubbish! If I had known he would make
such a ridiculous mess of the truth I would never have
invited him into my home."

"What did he say, Mother?"

"He says I *have* no spirit controls—that they are
merely figments of my own personality." She tossed
the magazine onto the table and rolled her eyes. "I
have gone over his secretary's transcripts! I have read
every single piece of information—all that I had no
earthly way of knowing! How could I have known of
his dead fiancé back in England? How could I have
known all those poor boys' last words to their mothers,
if not by some heavenly agency?" Her mother sat in her
customary attitude of frustrated exhaustion, cradling
her forehead in her long white fingers. "I suppose I
ought to write him," she sighed. "To thank him—but
for what, I can't imagine."

"I'll do it," Josie said. Her mother lifted her head
and cocked an eyebrow. "After all," she went on, "you're
terribly busy finishing your manuscript, and I do so
enjoy writing letters, and . . ." She was about to say *it's so
seldom I have a reason to,* but her mother might interpret
this as a veiled reference to Emily, and she desperately
needed to be allowed to pen this letter.

"Very well, then." Mrs. Clifford slid the magazine and accompanying letter across the table. "You may read the article before you compose your letter, but you must be succinct and polite but not at all flattering. You must show me the letter, and if it is not succinct and suitably reserved then I shall expect you to rewrite it."

The article wasn't nearly as condemnatory as her mother was making it out to be. There were several references that Josie did not understand—thanks to Emily, she had heard of Dr. Freud and Dr. Jung, but there were other names and terminologies that were unfamiliar to her.

But the crux of the article was perfectly clear. Dr. Jennings had indeed concluded that Mrs. Clifford's "spirit controls" were latent compartments of her own personality, which she employed as actors upon a metaphorical stage—but he also put forth the possibility that she had a genuine ability to "tap into the collective unconscious." There was too much information she could not have otherwise known.

Such supernatural knowledge was not proof of life beyond death, however, as the matter of Miss Eugenia Rice's letter attested. The doctor believed that Mrs. Clifford had been unable to summon the contents of the letter because no one in the room knew what it contained, that she had attempted a distraction by bizarrely mimicking a young male voice. Had she been able to communicate with the deceased Miss Rice, who had written the letter, then she could have proven it through a recitation of the missive inside its sealed envelope.

First Josie wrote the secret letter. Over the course of

four drafts, she discovered that what must be communicated need not always be said outright.

Dear Dr. Jennings,

I hope this letter finds you well. I am writing to ask you the greatest favor I feel I shall ever need to ask of anyone, and so I must first apologize for my boldness in doing so. I do not wish to burden you with the unpleasant details of our situation, so I will simply state that my sister's welfare depends upon our leaving our home.

I hope you will recall your introduction to our tutor, Miss Emily Jasper. She is the niece of Mr. Simon Jasper, editor-in-chief of the New York Evening Star. I would look to you always in deepest gratitude if you were to forward this letter to Emily in care of Mr. Jasper, for she is my best hope of making a better life for my sister and myself.

Sincerely yours,
Josie Clifford

The official thank-you letter, on the other hand, required only two drafts.

Dear Dr. Jennings,

Thank you for taking the time to forward your first article on the results of my mother's trance sessions. While I cannot say my mother is entirely satisfied with your conclusions, none of us can have any doubt whatever of your scientific integrity.

We shall eagerly await the publication of your

*second article, and thank you again for your kind-
ness.*

Sincerely yours,
Josie Clifford

She addressed the envelope and waited while her
mother read over the letter. Fortunately, she did not
give it much consideration, as she viewed the matter
of the thank-you note as an irritating distraction from
her manuscript. Mrs. Clifford handed her a two-penny
stamp before returning her attention to the typewriter.

The second letter was written and folded, biding
its time in her pinafore pocket. Alone in the hall, she
slipped both letters into the envelope and licked the seal
before leaving it on the mail table for Mrs. Pike to give
to the postman.

Back in the schoolroom, it occurred to her that she
could put her mind at ease if she were to hand the letter
to the postman herself. Generally he arrived while the
family was sitting down to luncheon, so she planned to
dally by a few minutes so she would be coming down
the stairs as the doorbell rang. She carried off this plan,
though her mother greeted her with sharp words when
she finally sat down to the meal. What did that matter?
It was accomplished.

The Beginning of Goodbye
34.

The dread crept up on him in ordinary moments, like when he glanced over his bookshelf and saw all the great novels he wouldn't have time to read to them; or when he looked up that book by Henry Rider Haggard at the library—the Victorian adventure novel that was one of Josie's favorites—and he knew he'd never try to explain to her why it was racist. He even felt the dread when he stood before the bathroom mirror brushing his teeth. It wasn't the same mirror, but hadn't she stood in this spot every night and done the same? "I found out," he said that night, once Cass had burrowed into bed. "I know."

His friend hesitated on the other side of the

horn . . . *Whose grave it is?*

He answered quickly, because she had been left to worry long enough: "It isn't yours and it isn't Cassie's."

Then whose . . . whose . . . A momentary silence fell over her side of the phonograph. *It's Mother's, isn't it?*

He didn't answer. He didn't have to.

You said there's no date on the stone. But you found the date in the records?

"Yes."

I won't ask.

"Like you said, it's better if you don't know too much."

When she spoke again her voice was thick with emotion. *Yes, I suppose you're right.*

"Are you crying?"

He heard her sniffle. *No.*

"It's okay if you are."

I know I shouldn't cry for her. I don't want *to cry for her.*

"It doesn't matter what she's said or done," Alec replied. "She's your mom. Of course you're going to feel sad." He paused. "Are you going to tell Cassie?"

No, she said firmly. *At least not for a long time.*

Then he told her about going to the town hall records office, and the theatrical flyer they'd found hidden in the scrapbook, and how Cass was bound to become a Broadway actress, although he didn't mention the name change. *I certainly won't tell her she's going to be famous,* Josie said. *She'll get a big head before she's done anything to warrant it!*

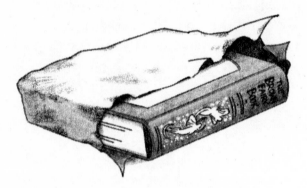

The Greatest of All Secrets
35.

The next two weeks were the longest of her life. Though Mr. Berringsley had taken the news of Othello's fate with surprising tranquility—"how was the child to know, Lavinia? I warned only you"—Mrs. Clifford had not finished punishing her younger daughter for the poor parrot's demise. Though she did not strike Cass again, their mother withheld even the meager love for which the girl so plainly yearned. Every dining-table conversation was a small agony of barbs and slights.

Josie's sense of relief at having sent the secret letter gave way to doubts and fears as the days passed. What if Dr. Jennings did not forward it? What if Emily's uncle did not approve of them asking her for aid? What if Emily herself was not in a position to help them? By the middle of the second week Josie was utterly convinced that their plan had failed, though she did not want to say as much to Alec. She and Cass made a little ceremony of placing the time capsule on the shelf in Emily's old cupboard, but it didn't cheer them much.

Faced with the prospect of remaining in the house on Sparrow Street for years to come, she felt the impulse to seek out her mother, to try to repair what she had played no part in rending. It made no sense, and yet she yielded to it, tiptoeing to the threshold of Mrs. Clifford's bedroom one sunny Sunday morning before breakfast.

The children had never been allowed beyond the boudoir, but a long oval mirror on an ornate stand of turned wood offered a glimpse of the four-poster bed, and once or twice Josie had stood in the ante-room doorway gazing into the glass at the exotic treasures within: the embroidered coverlet on the high stately bed, the framed portraits of distinguished strangers, the mahogany chest carved with cherubs and flowering vines.

The morning light streamed across the crumpled coverlet where her mother lay in her dressing gown of sapphire silk. The robe had come loose around her neck, and Josie could see the scars along Lavinia's collarbone. Merritt sat beside her at the foot of the bed. He wore no jacket, and her mother lifted a hand to finger the clip on his suspenders. "Oh, James," she murmured. "I am so tired."

James? It had never occurred to Josie that Merritt had a Christian name.

"I am so tired of this house. I am so tired of this *life.*" Her mother spoke wearily, and yet she seemed impossibly young all of a sudden, with her hair fallen loose across the lap of her manservant, and her pale eyes shining with unshed tears. "What if we went someplace . . . someplace far away from any war, or suffering, or discontent? Someplace where no one knows me, and no one would tug at my sleeve and ask for more, more, always more than I can give?"

It was impossible to think of her mother's beautiful face hidden so deep in the earth, and yet it *would* be. The tiny headstone was as clear in Josie's mind as if she'd traveled to the future to see it.

"You know I would follow you anywhere, Lavinia," Merritt answered in that toneless way of his, and the words seemed all the more sincere for their lack of passion. He lifted a broad white hand and began to stroke her hair, and she closed her eyes and sighed with pleasure. Josie backed away slowly, away from the mirror and out of the doorway. She did not want to see or hear any more.

At last, one bright Thursday afternoon in the middle of July, Mrs. Pike came into the dining room to hand Mrs. Clifford the mail. "There's a parcel for Miss Josephine." Mrs. Pike passed the brown-paper package to Mrs. Clifford with raised eyebrows. This was indeed cause for surprise, for the girls never, *ever* got mail. Josie's heart leapt into her throat.

Their mother inspected the return address. "That's strange. It's from Dr. Jennings."

The doctor had helped them! He must have, otherwise why would he send her anything at all? Mrs. Clifford, of course, opened the slim package instead of handing it to her as she ought to have done. It was a book, and along with it a letter. Before reading the note, Mrs. Clifford slipped the book back into the paper packaging, so that the girls could not see the cover. She opened the letter and proceeded to read it aloud over the remains of their chicken salad.

Dear Miss Clifford,

I shall always look back upon my visits to Edwardstown as a most stimulating and peculiar epoch in my career. I have, of course, even more questions now than when I began, but this is the nature of all forms of research, even on such mundane topics as geophysics or lepidoptery. I count myself among the most fortunate of men to have devoted my working days to a subject which is infinitely more interesting.

As a token of gratitude for your kindness and regard, I have enclosed a volume of stories for the enjoyment of yourself and your sister. The works of Mr. Andrew Lang are a favorite with my own niece and nephews.

Sincerely yours,
Henry Jennings

A book by their favorite author! How could it be a coincidence?

"A thank you for a thank you," Mrs. Clifford mused as she replaced the letter in its envelope. "You must have made quite an impression on him, Josephine."

By this stage, Josie was practically trembling with suspense. "You read the letter yourself, Mother. I don't recall that I wrote him anything to warrant such a lovely gesture."

Mrs. Clifford rolled her eyes as she poured herself a cup of tea. "I suppose now you must write him yet another thank you, and it will go on forever."

"May I see the book?"

Mrs. Clifford slid the package across the table and applied her dagger-shaped letter opener to the next envelope. "Marvelous news! Mr. Berringsley has shown the first three chapters of my manuscript to his associate at Harper and Brothers, and he says they plan to offer me a contract!" Already, Dr. Jennings's unexpected gift was stale news, and Josie couldn't have been more relieved.

She closed the nursery door and sat at the table before she allowed herself to look inside the package. It was *The Brown Fairy Book*. Cass frowned when she recognized the cover. "But we've already got the brown one!"

"Shh! Let me think." Josie opened the book and ran her fingers along the illustration on the title page. There must be a reason why Dr. Jennings had chosen it. *The Brown Fairy Book* was their favorite of the series, and Emily knew it.

She flipped through the pages until she reached "The Enchanted Head." There again was the illustration they loved: of the princess beside the throne where sat the sultan, her father, both of them staring down at the head of a man, fully animated, on a silver platter resting on the intricately tiled floor. Josie squinted, and turned the book sideways. Someone had written in pale pencil along the gutter, to the side of the illustration. It was Emily's hand. *We shall come for you on the last morning of July, just before five. Pack lightly but thoroughly, for I mean to keep you.*

Mrs. Dowd and Mrs. Pike were in the kitchen by half past five, even on Sundays, and the hall clock chimed on the hour, when her mother was most likely to be roused from sleep. Emily had thought of every-thing.

She handed the book to Cassie, and let her sound out the words herself. "If we leave Mother's house, there can be no coming back," Josie said. "Is this truly what you want, Cass?"

Her sister looked up from the book with shining eyes. "I knew we would be with Emily again. Mrs. Gubbins told me so."

Josie regarded her sadly. Cass was too young yet to be thinking of her keep, and who would earn it, and how. In her eyes this was such a simple decision. "But remember, you mustn't . . ."

"I know, I know. I mustn't speak of it to anyone but Alec."

It was the biggest secret they'd ever had to keep—bigger, even, than their friend from the future.

Not So Impossible After All
36.

The following night there was a knock at the door. Alec jumped, and whispered for the girls to be quiet as his mother was turning the knob. "I forgot to tell you, sweets—"

She frowned, listening through the hum and crackle of the rotating wax cylinder. Cass was saying, *What is it? Who's there? Are you still there, Alec?*, and Josie was shushing her.

"That . . ." she began uncertainly. "That can't be a record. Who is that?"

Please, please, please let her understand, he thought. He took a deep breath. "Josie."

She opened the door wide, shaking her head.

"Alec—"

"No, Mom. Just listen to me. This is real. I'm not making it up. Listen and see." He turned back to the phonograph and said, "Josie, are you still there?"

Yes, Alec. We're here. Are you . . . talking to your mother?

He could hear the hesitation in her voice. She was afraid his mom would take the phonograph away. "It's all right," he said. "I want Mom to hear you."

Hello, Mrs. Frost.

"Please, Mom." He beckoned her in. "Just say hello."

Slowly she came in and knelt on the carpet beside him, giving him a look he couldn't read. Then she leaned toward the mouth of the phonograph. "H-h-hello?"

It's Alec's mother! cried the first, younger voice. *Hello! How do you do?*

How do you do? echoed the other voice. *My name is Josie Clifford, and this is my little sister, Cassie.*

Cass, the first voice chirped. *My name is Cass. It's short for Cassandra, but I don't like to be called Cassandra or Cassie anymore.*

Sorry, said Josie. *Sometimes I forget.*

"It's . . . it's very nice to meet you." Mrs. Frost took a deep breath to steady herself, and when Alec reached for her hand she gripped it hard. "How old are you girls?"

I'm twelve and—

And I just turned seven!

"Oh, isn't that nice! Happy Birthday, Cass. Did you have a party?"

There was a brief silence, and, when the little girl spoke again, she was unusually reserved. *Mother wouldn't allow it.*

Mrs. Frost glanced at her son, and the thought was written on her forehead: *what kind of mother doesn't cele-*

brate her child's birthday? "Oh, I'm very sorry to hear that, Cass." She paused. "Josie, you said you're twelve? You're Alec's age."

Yes, ma'am. Alec turned twelve before I did, so he likes to think he's older. Josie's laughter came tinkling through the horn, and a smile cracked his mother's mask of apprehension.

"Alec told me . . . you live in our house. I mean— that is—"

That's true, Mrs. Frost, Josie said gently. *Someday it will be your house.* They heard Cass cough, and Josie went on: *We're using the phonograph in the same room. That's how we can hear one another so clearly. Alec and I figured it out.* Again his mother turned to look at him, her hand over her mouth. A light broke over her face. This room, her son's bedroom—it had once belonged to the girls.

They could hear Cass chattering on in the background. *Wouldn't it be nice if we could invite Alec and his mother and Danny for tea tomorrow? And Emily, too? It would be you and me and Alec and Mrs. Frost and Emily and Danny, all of us drinking Mr. Berringsley's tea that he had sent to us all the way from India in Mother's best china cups, and, oh yes, we would have those little cucumber sandwiches Mrs. Dowd only makes for important company.*

Yes, they heard Josie say to her sister. *That would be awfully nice. I wish they could all join us for tea.*

Alec's mother looked at him, reached again for his hand and squeezed it. In the dim light of his bedside lamp he could see unshed tears gleaming in the corners of her eyes.

Mrs. Frost?

"Yes, Josie?"

They could hear the girl hesitating on the far side of

the phonograph. *Do you believe him now?*

The morning was cool and rainy, so she made a pot of oatmeal with blueberries and maple syrup and coconut cream. Alec laid the rusted candy tin and shoebox of letters on the kitchen table, and she ran her finger down the stack of envelopes. "When you showed me that first letter, I *couldn't* believe you." She laid down her mug, crossed her arms over her chest and looked out the window at the gray morning. "That's what it means, being a parent. You can't believe in impossible things anymore. Everything is a matter of keeping you safe."

"I *am* safe."

"Not just safe in body, sweets. Safe and well in your mind, too. You showed me proof, but I couldn't see it. It just seemed more important than ever that you see Dr. D'Amato." She read the look on his face, and sighed. "You'll understand someday, if you have kids of your own. You can't just trust that everything's going to turn out all right. You have to make *sure* that it does."

Alec looked out the window and shivered. His mom might have been talking about the Clifford girls.

Now he told her everything—about the letters under the window seat, and how Josie would lock all the things in the spare-room cabinet especially for him, and all about Emily and Dr. Jennings and Lavinia Clifford herself. His mother cried when he got to the part about Cass being locked in the linen closet. "But I think I've been able to help them, Mom. They're . . ." He took a deep breath. "They're leaving with Emily. Three nights from now, they're leaving for good."

Goodnight, Forever
37.

Three nights became two. After midnight, letter in hand, Josie went down to her mother's study and switched on the desk lamp. Her heart thudded—anticipating another of Mrs. Clifford's pounces—and yet she knew she would not be caught, because Alec had found the letter in the archive.

There was a filing cabinet in the corner, the top drawer labeled *correspondence*. She opened the drawer, found a file toward the back marked *Clients, A-L*, and slipped the envelope inside. It was that simple.

Two nights became one, and once more she felt an urge to speak to her mother. It was half past ten, but a light still shone beneath the study door. Josie knocked, and heard a pause in the typewriter's clackety-clack. "Yes?"

"May I come in?"

"I suppose you'll barge in no matter what I say," her mother sighed, so she opened the door and went in.

"You're up late," Josie said.

"The editor at Harper and Brothers has asked me to make some changes to my manuscript," her mother replied. "What is it, Josephine?"

"Must I have a reason? Can't I simply wish you good night?" That dark image flashed in her mind, of the tiny gravestone in the cemetery on the hill. *If she opened her arms to me now, could we fix this? Could we change it, together?*

"If you've only come to wish me good night, then good night," her mother replied. "You know how important this book is to me—it will ensure my legacy—and you are quite old enough to understand how every interruption sets me back."

How foolish Josie had been to think that tonight, of all nights, she might reach her! If anything she could have done or said would have made a difference, then they would not be going away to begin with. "Good night, then, Mother."

The clacking of the typewriter resumed as she went out of the study and closed the door behind her. *I don't know when I'll see her again*, Josie thought as she climbed the stairs. *It might be months—or years—or never.* She locked the door from the inside, and packed her suitcase with one change of clothing along with the books Emily had left behind.

Josie lay awake, worrying of two things: that Merritt would prevent them from leaving, and—if they *were* able to leave—of their future keep. To Emily they were dear as sisters, but she could not expect her old friend to support them. She pushed from her mind all thoughts of Alec. Leaving her mother's house was the right thing to do, and she must take as much comfort in that conviction as she was able.

But she ought to have known it wouldn't be that easy. Sometime past midnight, wiping away tears, she rose and went to the phonograph. "Alec?" she whispered. "Alec, are you there?"

I'm here!

"I can't sleep."

Me neither. I don't know what I'm gonna do without you, Josie. It's so wrong to be saying goodbye to you like this, when I'll never see—I mean, speak to you again. He paused. *But you've gotta go. I know you do.*

"I'll write you." As she spoke she twisted the hem of her nightgown with trembling fingers. "Wherever I go, I'll find a safe place, and someday I'll tell you all about it."

There followed a moment of silence, laden with all the things he did not need to say: *I don't want any more letters. Letters aren't enough.*

What he said aloud was, *I wanted to tell you this earlier, only I was hoping it wouldn't be the last time we talked. I found out why there weren't any matches for Cassandra Clifford. She changed her name. That's why I couldn't find her before we found the playbill.*

Josie cast a glance at the bed across the room, where her sister lay sleeping in the tangled quilts. "What did she change it to?"

Jasper.

"You mean . . . they'll adopt her?"

I don't know for sure, but it looks that way. And there's one more thing. It's about you, Josie.

"I'm afraid to ask."

Your articles only go up to 1928. It makes me wonder if you end up doing something else.

Nineteen twenty-eight! She knew it would come eventually, and yet it seemed as likely as a masquerade ball on the ocean floor.

Whatever it is, Josie, I know you're gonna be amazing.

She almost laughed. "If we can get through the morning I'll consider it an accomplishment."

The clock in the hall struck four. *I know you have to go.*

She swallowed hard, but the lump in her throat would not pass. "I don't want to."

I don't want you to, either.

"It's easier for you, you know. You'll always be able to look for me, and you'll have my letters. But I won't ever know the first thing about what happens to you from now on."

I know, Josie. I know. I'd give anything to be able to write you.

"Will you remember me?"

I'll think about you every day.

She'd been so intent on the conversation that she was startled to notice Cass kneeling beside her, rubbing the sand from her eyes. "Mrs. Gubbins says you're taking real good care of her, Alec."

Cass? What are you doing up so early?

"We're going to live with Emily in the city."

Josie turned to her, her earlier resolution dissolved in a sudden fit of tenderness. "Alec says you're going to be a famous actress."

It twisted at her heart to see the look of pure delight on Cassie's face. "Really?"

"Shh!"

"Will I do Shakespeare, Alec? Will I be Juliet or Cordelia?"

"Anyone but Desdemona," Josie quipped.

I don't know about Shakespeare, but I'm sure you could if you wanted to. You're gonna be in a play called "The Comet Party."

"Am I the star?"

You sure are. Your picture's on the cover of the playbill. It'll be on at the Century Theatre and it was written by Byron Grimsby.

"Byron Grimsby?" Cassie wrinkled her nose. "What a silly name."

Someday you can tell Byron Grimsby I told you about his play before he even wrote it.

"It's time," Josie whispered. "We've got to say goodbye."

Write me a good long one, Josie. Write me a letter I can always reread.

She made no attempt to wipe away her tears as she slotted the wax cylinder in the box, tucked in the bedclothes, and finished gathering her things. It did not occur to her to leave her bed unmade, for Mrs. Pike would find enough fault with the rest of their actions. On her pillow she left the note she'd written that evening:

Dear Mother,

> *We have gone to live with Emily. You may be angry with us, but I suspect that it will be a relief to see us go. I will always be grateful to you for my life, and for the comfort and opportunity with which you provided us.*

Your daughter,
Josie

"I'm ready." Cass stood in the center of the room with her suitcase in one hand and Mrs. Gubbins clutched tightly in the crook of her arm.

"What are you doing?" Josie went for the doll, but Cass pulled it out of reach.

"I can't leave her here!"

"But you can't bring her, Cass!" Josie pointed through the spare-room doorway. "Don't you see? It's already done!"

Cassie paused as she always did—as if she were listening to the doll. "But you're my friend," she whispered.

"If we take her with us Alec will never find her in the cupboard," said Josie, shifting her suitcase from one hand to the other. It was fast coming up on five o'clock.

Reluctantly Cass followed Josie into Emily's old room and watched as Josie opened the cupboard door and placed the doll on the shelf beside the time capsule. "Yes. I understand. Good bye, Mrs. Gubbins. I'll never forget you."

Josie closed the cupboard door, and hesitated. Should she take the key? She looked down at Cass, who gazed back with wide somber eyes. Josie dropped the key in her pocket.

At five minutes to five the girls knelt at the reading-room window, peering out at the darkened street. Their pasteboard suitcases were waiting by the door. Josie reached for her sister's hand and squeezed it hard.

"I hope they come soon," Cass whispered. "I feel about ready to bletch."

"I'm sorry about Mrs. Gubbins."

Cass shrugged and gave her a tiny smile. "She's Alec's now." A moment later Josie watched her face light up. Cass pressed her finger to the windowpane.

"Look!"

A motorcar stood idling at the curb on the opposite side of the street. Josie felt herself rising to her feet, taking her sister's hand, tiptoeing into the hall, and gathering the suitcases before they closed the front door for the last time. It seemed to her that they floated, not ran, to the strange auto waiting at the far curb. Emily, dressed in black, opened the back door and reached for their suitcases.

Josie couldn't see who was in the driver's seat; he only whispered something to Emily that Josie didn't catch. As the motorcar turned the corner onto Hemlock Street, Cass buried her face in Emily's bosom with a strangled cry of elation. Josie turned to look at the house through the back window. No tall dark figure had followed them onto the front walk this time, but a light was shining in her mother's bedroom, and she could clearly see Merritt's form like a sentinel at the window, his massive hand holding back the curtain. She felt a cold trickle down the back of her neck. He had *let* them leave.

Then Emily took her hand, and she turned around and settled herself on the seat. "Josie, Cass: I would like you to meet my uncle Simon, master of intrigue!"

With a chuckle, Uncle Simon took one hand off the wheel to tip his hat. "There'll be plenty of time for how-do-you-do once we're back in Manhattan," he said as they turned onto the road that would take them most of the way there. "Not to mention breakfast. Just wait 'til you see the meal Nora's cooking up. She's beside herself waiting to meet you girls."

"I hope there's bacon," Cass whispered, and Emily laughed as Josie shushed her. There was a momentary silence, which Josie filled with an anxious thought for all the trouble the Jaspers were about to take on their account.

Once again Emily took her hand. "Don't worry, dear. Everything will be fine. I've thought it all through." She sighed. "I wrote you every day for a month, you know. I don't suppose she ever let you read them."

Josie shook her head.

"None of that matters now though," Emily said contentedly as Cass laid her head in her lap. "Well, my dears. We always said one day we would have an adventure."

There Is More Than One Kind of Happy Ending
38.

Alec found out after the girls were gone that his mother had bought the phonograph from Mr. Penhallow, and it only occurred to him years later—on a wintry weekday morning, deep in the stacks of a university library—that the version of her future he'd found in the archives was the future he'd helped her make. Everything might have turned out differently had she asked him not to look. After Josie and Cass were gone he went through a period of wanting to find out almost everything there was to know of their lives, and listening to his iPod recordings of their conversations over and over. But all that ended with the discovery of Josie's obituary.

A wise man once observed that you aren't aware you have any illusions until they're taken from you; and until he saw her name along with "died last week at her home" in stark black and white, he hadn't realized he'd been nursing a wild and ridiculous hope that he and Josie could somehow build a bridge across the years that separated them. All along he'd dreamed she'd come walking out of his closet in her dress with the puffed sleeves, and she would know him instantly even though she had never seen his face.

For what felt like hours he stared at the microfilm screen. Josephine Clifford, 62, author and journalist; previously the secretary and assistant to Dr. Thomas Stapleton, distinguished professor of archaeology at Columbia University and one of the world's foremost experts on pre-Incan civilizations; accompanied the professor on expeditions in Bolivia, Ecuador, and Peru; had been engaged to marry the professor when he was tragically killed in an automobile collision outside Lima. Survived by her sister, the actress Cassandra Jasper, and extended family.

This was why he'd never wanted to dig too deep. An illusion may not be real, but it can be awfully comforting.

A recent portrait accompanied the obituary. When she died she'd been only a few years younger than Grammy Sal. Though he could still see the girl he'd known in the face on the screen, he felt himself inching away from her, distracted and confused by all the facts that were unfamiliar to him. Josie, give up her journalism career to follow some stuffy professor all the way to Peru? Josie, engaged to marry a man almost old enough to be her father?

His mother told him people don't ever really

change—but she'd been talking about his dad, and that wasn't true of everyone. *No*, Alec thought as he closed the browser window and shut down the computer. *They only change when you don't want them to.*

That summer Alec's mother started dating a man she'd met at the farmers' market. At first it felt strange to see her happy again, to realize that there was a whole secret room in her heart that no amount of love from him could open.

But this new life was, in many ways, far better than the old. Steve laughed loudly and often, he helped Alec with his science projects, and, when the time came, he proofread Alec's college application essays and taught him how to drive a stick. Steve loved the old house on Sparrow Street as much as they did, and he came home in time for dinner every single night.

Alec and Danny remained the best of friends. In eighth grade they started acting classes on Saturday mornings, and in the beginning, Alec passed many anxious moments in front of the mirror in the boys' bathroom. Danny was a natural, but what made *him* think he could stand up in front of a bunch of strangers and convince them he was somebody else?

Then he thought of Cass, and Josie, and how brave they had been to follow through on something that at first had felt impossible. He took a deep breath whenever the old fear rose up in him, and while he'd never be as fine an actor as his friend, he was still pretty good, and once he forgot his anxiety he really enjoyed it. When they got to high school they starred together in every fall play and spring musical: Curley and Will, Puck and Bottom, the Tinman and the Scarecrow.

It was this new interest that eventually led him back to the Clifford sisters. Danny was studying theater and art history at NYU, and Alec would take the train down from Syracuse on long weekends to visit his friend. One day, Danny, with that impish air of his, handed Alec an antique playbill. *A KISS TO BORROW, at the Century Theatre. Written and directed by Byron F. Grimsby. Starring Algernon Trimble and Cassandra Jasper.*

On the cover, a girl in a frothy gown pointed an accusing finger at a surprised-looking man in a dinner jacket. *Cass.* "Where did you find this?"

"One of those memorabilia stores up around Broadway." His friend reached out and tapped the name of the writer-director. "They were married. Did you know that?"

"Who—Cass and Grimsby?"

"Yeah. I was wondering why she starred in so many of his plays, so I looked them up. Married forty years, until he died of lung cancer. One daughter."

In a dark room in his mind Alec heard her say, *Byron Grimsby? What a silly name!*

"Josie told you she'd write you again. Don't you want that letter?"

Alec thought of the cupboard key inside the padded envelope, the Upper West Side address printed neatly in a not-yet-grownup hand at the top left corner. Whoever sent it had *wanted* him to come.

But he couldn't just take the subway uptown, find the apartment building and press the buzzer. He wasn't ready for it to be that easy, because the memory of his friend's death notice threw a chill over his heart whenever he thought of it. So he began with Byron Grimsby, whose family had donated his archive to the New York Public Library. There, on summer vacations and visits to Danny or his father, he read all the plays Byron F. Grimsby had ever written.

Some time later, he and Danny wandered into one of those Broadway nostalgia shops, and were struck dumb by the blue-and-silver poster hanging high above the counter. *THE MAN FROM TOMORROW*, it said. *Written and directed by Byron F. Grimsby. Starring Cassandra Jasper and Bartholomew Stark.* The leads embraced at the center of the poster before a backdrop of the constellations. Cass wore a sleeveless, vaguely Grecian gown, and her co-star was dressed in shoulder-to-toe black, with a spiky haircut—so incongruous in the 1920s. "I don't care what it costs," Danny whispered. "You *have* to buy it."

"That was Grimsby's most successful play," said the man behind the counter, who wore thick black eyeglasses and a *Young Scrappy & Hungry* t-shirt. "Ever heard of it?"

Alec didn't tell the man behind the counter that he had taken Grimsby's typewritten manuscript (complete with notes and revisions in red grease pencil) out of a cardboard folio, read it hungrily and traced his fingertip over a crinkly coffee stain on the title page. He wanted to pretend he was hearing the story for the first time.

Danny understood and shook his head. "What's it about?"

"The girl meets a guy who dresses and acts and talks a little strangely, and eventually he tells her he's from the future. She's all conflicted, right? Is he a time traveler or a lunatic? So of course all her friends and family think he's nuts, but she begins to believe him. And in the last scene, in her parents' living room, she disappears with him in a blinding flash of light." As he spoke the man's face was transfixed, as if he were recounting the scene from memory.

"If I didn't know better," said Danny, "I'd think you'd actually seen it."

The man laughed. "I wish! Nah, I just read some reviews on microfilm. The really wild thing is how Grimsby imagined the future. There's no tinfoil or any of the other wacky things you find in those early sci-fi dramas. His hero wears a backpack—just like one from L.L. Bean, you know?—and he's always carrying this tablet that sounds a lot like an iPad. Way ahead of its time."

Alec felt the corner of his mouth twitching. "I guess it must have been."

"Hah." The man pointed a *gotcha* finger. "Hah, hah. Right." He turned, arms folded, and took another moment to admire the poster. "Anyway, yeah. I've thought of buying it myself."

"Why didn't you?"

"I've pretty much run out of room on my walls. I'm too often tempted, working here."

It did not matter that the poster cost three hundred and seventy-five dollars. Alec handed over his credit card.

Every so often he kissed a girl, took her to the movies or out for Indian food, but after a few days he found his heart wasn't in it. Over time he became the butt of his college friends' good-natured jokes. One time a guy he wasn't even close to remarked, "Alec's looking for the kind of girl they don't make anymore." *Funny*, he thought, *how someone who doesn't know you sees more than you'd expect.*

Once he'd read everything of Byron's—he'd come to

think of the playwright by his first name—he turned, almost unwillingly, to Josie's memoir, for which he filled out a call slip in the main reading room of the New York Public Library. The opening chapters told of her stormy upbringing at the hands of Lavinia Clifford, her adoption by the Jaspers, and of her rise in the ranks of the *New York Evening Star* alongside Cassie's early years in show business. Mindful that her sister was following in their mother's footsteps, she traced Lavinia's career to its beginning, and wrote of the meetings she'd had with some of the stagehands and chorus girls who'd once asked Lavinia for messages from their departed loved ones.

She wrote, too, of coming back to Edwardstown for her mother's funeral in 1927.

> *We were all grown up; no one recognized us, and so we overheard far more than we wanted to. With clucking tongues and gasps of horror the ladies of Edwardstown told each other that Lavinia Clifford had drunk herself to death, and that with so many bad investments there was hardly enough money left even to pay the servants' pensions. And what had become of her silent manservant, who never seemed to age? Either he had left her in her final hours, or he was hiding in the house behind those heavy black draperies.*
>
> *If we were to judge by the volume of gossip in the shops and the hotel dining room where we took our meal that evening, we expected we'd see a fine crowd in the church the following day, but at the service it was only myself, Cass, Emily, the servants, and two or three clients who had believed in our mother to the very end. We'd overheard at*

the hotel that Lavinia had fallen out with Berr-
ingsley some years before, which prepared us for
his absence at the funeral. It was a relief that we
did not see him. Coming face to face after so many
years with Mrs. Pike and Mrs. Dowd, who'd never
been kind to us, was awkward enough.

They hadn't seen their mother in the intervening years, and she'd contacted them only through her lawyer to release the trust accounts her late husband had established for the girls' financial security. On occasion, she and Cass had both written to her, sending newspaper clippings that proved their accomplishments, but she'd never replied.

It stung that she should recount her childhood at great length without ever mentioning the talking board or phonograph. When he reached the section on her life and adventures with Dr. Stapleton, he stopped reading. He didn't know if he'd ever feel ready for that part.

He brooded over all this until Danny put him straight. "She couldn't write about you, man! People would think she was crazy." They were on the phone, and Alec could hear him chewing something as he talked. "And she *did* write about you. Got her brother-in-law to, anyway. Haven't you dithered long enough?"

Danny was right. It was time to write a letter to whomever lived on West 87th Street.

Of course, he'd memorized the address the very day the key arrived in the mail. Someone in the apartment pressed a button to let him in, and he passed through an Art Deco hallway of black marble and gilded trim into a narrow elevator. Part of him wanted to run from this, to put it off for a few more years. There could be no more letters, no second reunion with these strangers who knew all about him.

He stepped out of the elevator and a door opened at the end of the hall. For a second—just one second, and then it passed—he saw Josie in a striped sweater and gray corduroys, her wild dark hair pulled back from her face in a hasty chignon, careless and elegant at the same time. The long straight nose, the warm, earnest expression—she was Josie, and a moment later she was not.

"It's you? You're Alec?" He nodded, and when she smiled that buried wish tore at his heart. "Amazing, isn't it? I could've sat next to you on the subway and I would never have known you." For a long moment they stood looking at each other on either side of the doorway.

Finally the girl held out her hand. "I'm Nora. Cass's great-granddaughter. Come in. My grandmother—Emily Jane—she's in the living room."

The apartment was well lived in, with pictures and paintings on the corridor walls and shelves lined with old hardcovers. The air smelled faintly of a spice he couldn't identify. An old woman sat in an armchair by a window, eyes closed, smiling into the afternoon sunshine. There was a plate of hummus and crackers and a pitcher of iced tea with two glasses on a table at her elbow.

Nora looked down at the packet in his hand. "Are those . . . the letters?" He nodded and handed her the cache of envelopes. "I'll be very careful with them," she whispered. "Thank you." He looked back to Emily Jane and saw the thick, yellowed envelope in her gnarled hands.

The girl made as if to leave, then turned in the

doorway, hesitating. "I used to ask for bedtime stories about the boy from the future. I always wanted to find you—after all, we knew where you lived!—but Gran said you'd come to us when you were ready." She flushed as she made this confession.

"I'm sorry it took me so long," he replied, with the ghost of a smile. She smiled back, and went out of the room as he approached the figure in the chair.

Emily Jane opened her eyes. "So it's you, at last. The boy from tomorrow."

He sat down beside her. "Your mother named you after Emily?"

"Oh, yes. The Jaspers raised them, you know. She was my aunt Em." The woman's chin trembled, and her eyes filled with tears. But she made an effort to compose herself and gave him a shrewd look. "I imagine you know a little of what it feels like—remembering those who are gone."

He nodded. "Thank you for meeting me, Mrs. Newman."

"Oh, do call me Emily Jane. You were always Alec to me." She sighed fondly. "When I was a child my mother read me *The Little Prince*, and she told me you'd read it to her first, on her seventh birthday. Then I learned the meaning of the word 'impossible,' and also that I could never rightly use it." Emily Jane paused, remembering. "She wrote a letter to the author, you know. To warn him his plane would be shot down during the war. He probably never received it, poor man—not that he would have believed her, anyway. Would anyone? But all that is in the letter, I expect. Aunt Josie always wrote the most interesting letters, didn't she?" He nodded, smiling, and she held out the envelope. "I know you've waited a long time for this—

not as long as I have, but long enough. I think I'll take a nap while you read it."

She settled back into the armchair and closed her eyes, but he did not open the letter right away. This was the very last of them and must be savored more than any other. The window looked out over a staggered gray patchwork of roofs, and beyond them he could see the greenery of Central Park. Alec looked around the room, at the framed photographs and knick-knacks arranged on the end-tables. He saw Cass and Byron with Emily Jane on his lap—Josie in her late twenties, dressed in the windswept garb of a girl adventurer—and Emily and her husband with their own three children. He looked down at the envelope in his hands, not so faded as those that had come before it: *Mr. Alec Frost.*

The letter was dated December 31, 1949, and it answered all his questions, even the ones he hadn't wanted to put into words. Her handwriting had changed, but he wouldn't linger on that. He'd rather think of her as a twelve-year-old girl recounting a dream she'd had of her future life.

She wrote of how her tutor had written to the New York Society for the Prevention of Cruelty to Children on their behalf, of the early morning Emily and her uncle came for them in the car at five o'clock, and how she'd worried they would be a burden to their new family.

Mother allowed us the money Father Clifford had set aside, and it was far and away the kindest thing she ever did for us. Still, I fretted that the money, all of it, rightfully belonged only to Cass, and it did not matter that Aunt Nora and Uncle Simon treated us like the children they'd never had.

I always had the nagging feeling that I should begin earning my living as soon as I could, and I did. You were right, Alec. When I was sixteen I started as a secretary at the Evening Star, taking night classes at Hunter College for my B.A.; within two years I was a weekly contributor to the ladies' page, and the year after that they sent me on my first real assignment. I can't tell you what a thrill it was to see my name in print, at least in the beginning.

She described Emily's husband Jack, who ran his own news service, slept in a cubby-hole for ten minutes at a time and drank two gallons of coffee a day, and how Cass kept the theatrical awards she'd collected over the years in a row across the mantel of a painted-over fireplace. These were little pieces of history he'd never find on microfilm.

I wish you could have seen her on stage and off it too. She will always be the same feisty little imp. Even now I watch her learning her lines and think of how she used to stick out her tongue on the side of her mouth whenever she pressed pencil to paper.

I must tell you about Byron. He is the sort of man who helps an elderly person cross the street or gives a significant sum of money to a friend in need and mentions it to no one. He is also the sort who would laugh when I recounted your "prediction" that Cass would one day work with a man named Byron F. Grimsby, and how she made fun of his name. He has been a kinder brother than I ever could have hoped for.

Cass was seventeen when they met. She'd agreed

to an unpaid role in a college production as a favor for a friend, and Byron was the playwright and director, a student at New York University. I remember the evening he discovered our connection to Lavinia Clifford. His grandmother had been a devoted Spiritualist in her day, and he'd grown up hearing stories of all the impossible things our mother had said and done in her illustrious career. He was so enthralled, so eager, that I had to leave the room.

By then we were living on our own, in an apartment just across the hall from Emily and Jack, and in the evenings I sat at my typewriter while Cass learned her lines. I would fall asleep listening to her murmuring to people who were not there, and I inevitably thought of the past.

And of course, there was *The Man From Tomorrow*. Cass wanted Byron to name the hero after you, but he said "Alec" was too old fashioned, it wouldn't be convincing.

. . . Do you remember my telling you of those times when Mother made that terrible prediction in her trance state—that one of us would betray her? Well, Byron wrote a play about it: the rise and fall of a psychic medium. Mother's fictional counterpart had no children, and Byron gave her another name, but it was undeniably Mother.

By then they were married, and Byron had always intended Cass for the starring role. I never let her hide with me in the back hallway outside the reading room, yet it was as if she'd watched through the keyhole just as I had. She *was* Mother, down to the languid lolling of the head, the booming voice of the "spirit control," the twitching *of the long white fingers. It was difficult to watch, and indeed it was the only one of Cassie's plays I did not see more than once.*

In a sense, then, Mother's prophecy had come true. Yet if she had shown the poor child some love and kindness, no such prediction would have ever passed her lips. I suppose you know, library detective that you are, that her memoir was never published. I did not even find a copy in her personal papers. But I've said well enough on this subject, haven't I? My mother cannot defend herself, nor can she repent. I can only wish her peace.

Now I must tell you of Dr. Jennings. Once we were settled with Emily's aunt and uncle at their apartment in Chelsea, all five of us met our dear psychical researcher for lunch at the Hotel Knickerbocker, which was quite a treat. The doctor was in fine form, having recently exposed a fraudulent medium who'd been doing sittings for war widows, and I remember that our conversation was full of laughter and fascinating anecdotes. "These girls are much changed since the last time I met them," he remarked to Uncle Simon. "There is a light in their eyes which ought to have been there always." How sorry I was when it came time to shake his hand and quit the restaurant! I'd taken for granted that we would see him again, but the years passed quickly, and it was Uncle Simon who broke the news that the doctor had collapsed on the squash court. You did not tell me when he would die, but I thought of you on that day. It was September, 1919. There were so many people at the funeral that we were obliged to stand in the back.

*I want you to know that I often think of the
kindness and concern you showed for us in those
lonely days before Dr. Jennings made it possible for
us to leave. It still stuns me to know that it was I
who decided not to have her name added to Father
Clifford's stone, I who arranged for the bramble
bush to be planted beside the grave, I who decided
we should not be named among her survivors, and
I who started the deed of 444 Sparrow Street into
the succession of hands that would ultimately lead
me to you.*

Sounds from the kitchen tugged him out of her
narrative, and for a few moments he watched Cassie's
daughter as she slept. He thought of the letter the little
girl had written him after they could no longer communicate through the talking board—*I hope I live to be a
very old wumman so you can come and visit me wen I am
very old*—and the memory gripped his heart like a vise.
Not exactly, Cass.

*Will it be Emily Jane who has given you
this letter? Was it she who sent you the key to
the cupboard? I have told her all about you, of
course—and she has promised, with the gravitas
of a Templar knight, to keep it safe in the meantime. As I write this she is eighteen, and about
to leave for her first New Year's Eve party at the
Starlight Ballroom. I am staying with Cass and
Byron tonight, and, from where I sit at the spare
room desk, I can see Emily Jane standing in front
of the bathroom mirror in her high heels, smiling
to herself as she applies her lipstick. She has a young
man in her life, a naval officer. One time during*

the war, poor boy, he went for over a year without setting foot on land. I wish you could see her, Alec; she has more than a little of her mother's panache. How old is she now?...

The phone rang, and it startled him out of the letter. For a moment or two this sensation lingered—of being yanked out of another time and place—but the scent of frying onions wafting from the kitchen returned him to the present.

Emily Jane was awake now. "You're still reading," she observed. "But then, I suppose that's the longest letter anybody ever wrote you."

He nodded. "I think I'll finish it later, if you don't mind."

Nora appeared in the doorway, twisting a dish towel in her pale hands. "We were hoping you'd stay for dinner."

"I'd love to," he replied, a little too quickly. Emily Jane grinned, and he felt his heart clutch again as the impish face of her mother shone out through the wrinkles. It was gone a moment later, but Alec went on smiling. He turned to Nora. "Do you need any help?"

"Sure," she said. "If you feel like chopping some vegetables. I'm just making a stir fry."

She led him into the narrow kitchen, the counters and cabinets awash in golden afternoon light. "It was you, wasn't it?" Alec managed to ask. "You sent the key?"

Nora laid down a knife and a yellow pepper. She met his eye, and nodded. There was a look on her face, sad and hopeful, and full, too, of some other feeling neither of them would be able to identify for a little while yet.

Meanwhile, None of This
Has Even Happened Yet
39.

*For years I only thought of writing. I imagined
hiding letters in places I knew you'd never find:
at the back of a cupboard in our apartment near
Washington Square, or under the floor-boards in a
Vienna hotel room. When Tom died, and then all
through the war, I told myself that I must write,
but something kept me from it. I hope you will
understand, Alec: I knew I should not live my life
with my head caught in a future I can play no part
in.*

Josie laid down her pen and stretched her fingers. Cass came down the hall and poked her head in. "We'll leave for Martino's at nine-thirty. Byron's made the reservation for ten."

Martino's on Mulberry Street was their New Year's tradition. The streets of Little Italy were just as festive as Times Square but much less frenetic. Josie nodded, smiled, and turned back to her letter, thinking Cass would not linger. "Who are you writing to?"

Josie looked up from the desk, and when she spoke she heard the catch in her voice. "Our old friend Alec."

Her sister's eyes lit up. "That's marvelous, Josie! You mean you still write to him?"

"I don't, really. I tried once or twice, but it simply wouldn't come as easily as it did then."

"That's only natural. You were children, and now you're a grown woman writing to a child."

"That's just it," said Josie. "I'll never know how old he'll be when he reads this. He could be twelve, or twenty, or fifty . . ."

Cass asked, "How are you planning to leave it for him?"

Before Josie could reply, Emily Jane's voice sang out from the bathroom down the hall. "Mother, may I borrow your eyeliner?"

Cass turned in the spare-room doorway and called, "Absolutely not. That make-up's for the stage, do you understand? I will not have you plastering your face like a vaudeville chorus girl." She turned back to her sister. "Now, what was I just asking you?"

Josie grinned. "You were asking to whom I'm planning to entrust the letter."

Cass lifted her eyebrows and glanced back at her daughter framed in the yellow bathroom light, then sat heavily on the bed. "I can't think of how old she'll be in 2016. Good grief, Josie! I'll be cold in the ground."

Josie patted Cass on the knee. "Which is why I'm leaving it with her instead of you."

The sisters looked at each other and laughed. "Well," said Cass, after a moment. "I'll let you write. Tell him I still think of him fondly."

Cass came into the room just now, and we spoke of you. She thinks of you often and asked me to tell you so.

I've tried to think of all the questions you'd ask me if you could, and there's one question I find myself reluctant to answer. There are two periods of my life that I look back on with the greatest fondness, even though they were times fraught with uncertainty: there is you, of course, and there is Tom. I wish you could have known him, Alec—he often reminded me of you with his insatiable curiosity, his delight in a good book, his unwillingness to give up in the face of frustrating circumstances.

Do you recall Mrs. Gubbins's prophecy that I would never marry? We were digging for potsherds one gray October morning when Tom turned to me and, without any fuss or ceremony, asked me to be his wife. We'd always been very much at ease with one another, and I suppose I could characterize my feelings for him as a fierce sort of affection. I had no visions of a honeymoon on the Riviera, or a house with a white picket fence; no, the only thing I thought of was Mrs. Gubbins, and how I cried myself to sleep that night, and how Cass apologized for telling me what was meant to be a secret. That was what had shaken me so at the time: when Cass has a conviction, you can be sure it is not rooted in any sort of fantasy or wishful thinking.

So when Tom asked me to marry him—how ashamed I am to admit this!—the first thing I thought was, "That stupid dirty old doll was wrong. I'll marry him and <u>prove</u> her wrong." Tom had the heart of a scientist, and I managed to convince myself he loved me only as I loved him, that he too saw our marriage as a comfortable arrangement.

For the past ten years I've carried this guilt, because part of me believes that had I done the honest thing and denied him, Tom would be alive today. I wonder if Mrs. Gubbins ever talks to you the way she spoke to Cassie; I wonder if she's already told you what I've done. I didn't want to think she could be real, not even when she spoke to me in the middle of the night, but I see the folly in that now. It makes no sense to believe in you and not her.

You guessed I would change careers, and Tom had everything to do with that too. He came into the Evening Star offices one day for an interview—fresh off his discovery of the Señora de Supe, the mummified priestess with the priceless golden breastplate, and even the popular papers and magazines were eager to write of her—and as he sat down on the far side of my desk a strange feeling settled over me, rather like that which accompanied our early sessions on the talking board. I should preface this by saying I was twenty-seven years of age and had already been working at the newspaper for a decade. Most days I felt I'd written every story there was to tell.

For an hour he told me about his life, from his boyhood explorations in a Roman rubbish pit to his latest field-work in a desert by the sea. As he stood up and shook my hand he said, "Come with me to Peru, if you like. I'm in need of an assistant." In that instant a new life unfurled before me, like the flag of a brand-new nation. I hope you'll have plenty of those moments in your own life, Alec . . .

Emily Jane came floating into the room on a cloud of jasmine. "All right, Aunt Jo—I'm off."

Josie offered her cheek to be kissed. "Be good."

"I'm always good," her niece retorted.

Josie raised an eyebrow, and Emily Jane laughed as she glided out the door. A moment later the clock struck nine, and Josie rose from her desk. She could finish the letter tomorrow.

"Do you know what Josie was doing this evening?" said Cass as the assembled diners—Josie, Byron, Jack and Emily—perused the wine list. "She was writing a letter to the very person to whom you owe your fame and fortune."

Byron waggled his bushy gray eyebrows. "Ah, but that would be you, my lovely."

"Why would she be writing a letter to *me*, you silly man? No, she was writing to *Alec*."

Byron's eyes grew wide. "Alec? Really?"

"That's what *I* said. Isn't it splendid?"

Emily was excited too. "Did you tell him about Byron's play?"

Josie nodded. "But if I know him, he'll have already heard of it. Alec loved poking through the library

256

archives."

"Funny to think of my work going in an archive," said Byron. "The play isn't *that* old."

"It's been twenty years since you wrote it," Cass pointed out.

"Speaking of which, how's the new play coming along?" Jack asked, and they were off on another train.

Byron ordered an outrageously expensive bottle of prosecco for the table—of course the war had interfered with wine production, and prices had been high ever since—and when it arrived he poured them each a glass. "May I make the toast?" he asked, and everyone agreed. "To Alec," Byron said. "The man from tomorrow!"

Something occurred to Josie as her dear ones clinked their flutes, and the realization left her with a feeling of serenity. Their discovery, their secret, their impossible friendship: it was all still ahead of him. She raised the glass to her mouth, smiling to herself as she took the first sip.

A Word of Advice

The characters' use of the talking board in this story allows them to form a friendship across time, but if you attempt to use such a device in real life your experience may be very different. Horror stories are only entertaining when they happen to other people, and so the author recommends you leave the talking board to the realm of fiction.

Acknowledgments

Seanan McDonnell (first and best reader), Alonzo Jennings, Nova Ren Suma, McCormick Templeman, Mackenzi Lee, McKelle George, Marika McCoola, Kendall Kulper, Rebecca Mahoney, Elizabeth Duvivier, Amiee Wright, Todd Noaker & Bill Mullen, Ailbhe Slevin & Christian O'Reilly, Deirdre Sullivan & Diarmuid O'Brien, Victoria Moran, Kelly Brown, Aravinda Seshadri, Keith Godbout, Joelle Renstrom & James Miller, as well as Mary Bonina, Debka Colson, Kate Gilbert, Susan Tan, Alexander Danner, and all my friends at the Writers' Room of Boston. I am grateful to Mary Lee Donovan for showing me exactly how to fix what wasn't working, to Agnieszka Grochalska for her perfect illustrations, to Kayla Church, Dayna Anderson, Keara Donick, and Cami Wasden at Amberjack for being so thoroughly delightful to work with, and to Barney Karpfinger and Cathy Jaque at the Karpfinger Agency for their support. Thanks most of all to Kate Garrick for her optimism and determination, and to my family (particularly my sister Kate) for inspiring this story in the first place. Olivia and Quinn, I hope you've enjoyed it.

About the Author

Camille DeAngelis is the author of several novels for adults—each of them as full of impossible things as *The Boy From Tomorrow*—as well as a travel guide to Ireland and a book of nonfiction called *Life Without Envy: Ego Management for Creative People*. Her young adult novel *Bones & All* won an Alex Award from the American Library Association in 2016. Camille loves knitting, sewing, yoga, and baking vegan cupcakes. She lives in New England. Visit her online at www.cometparty.com.

About the Illustrator

Agnieszka Grochalska lives in Warsaw, Poland. She received her MFA in Graphic Arts in 2014. Along the way, she explored traditional painting, printmaking, and sculpting, but eventually dedicated her keen eye and steady hand to drawing precise, detailed art reminiscent of classical storybook illustrations. Her current work is predominantly in digital medium, and has been featured in group exhibitions both in Poland and abroad.

She enjoys travel and cultural exchanges with people from around the world, blending those experiences with the Slavic folklore of her homeland in her works. When she isn't drawing or traveling, you can find her exploring the worlds of fiction in books and story-driven games. Agnieszka's portfolio can be found at agroshka.com.